The Storms

Transient

Dominic Took

The Storms of Acias

Transient Imprint
Transient Innovations Ltd
Staffordshire University Business Village Stoke
72 Leek Road
Stoke-on-trent
Staffordshire
ST4 2AR, UK
Tel: (+44) 0844 8845190
E-mail: contact@transientinnovations.co.uk
Web: www.transientinnovations.co.uk

ISBN 978 0 9556123 0 5

Transient is an imprint of Transient Innovations Ltd

For all those that never stopped believing in a dream, to make that dream a finer future for all.

1

Graciou's eyes flicked across the dark brown horizon outside of the classroom window. The sky was billowing outward toward him and his school, slowly darkening into a brown mass.

Every few seconds his teacher's words would break through, bringing him back to reality.

"Graciou? Where were the first cornerstones placed?" she said, trying to bring him back to the topic of the class.

He stared outside toward the horizon, the now billowing brown cloud turning into several more clouds, each jutting out from underneath it.

"At the four points upon the horizon…"

He knew the answer only too well and it bore him no pain to say it. He could hear her voice turning away to the others in the class, instantly leaving him to further explore his view. Suddenly, a large chunk of brown rock fell out of the now darkening cloud formation, rocketing upward and then sloping back down before his eyes. Distracted by it, he hadn't noticed his teacher, her face now white with fear, at the cloud that was forming.

"Children, exit the classroom quickly. Wait outside!"

He heard a brief pause, as he was watching the now small pieces of rock that were shooting out from the base of the cloud.

"Graciou move outside with the others!" she shouted over at him.

He got up with a start and walked over to form up behind his other classmates.

"Children pair up with each other and follow your headmistress," her voice started to sound all the more anxious.

Still watching the windows at the edge of his view, he could see the cloud moving across the top half of the window, pieces of rock still falling closer and closer toward them all. He felt his hand snatched from his side and his gaze broken, as he was spun round. The children that had been lined up had already paired and followed their headmistress down into the bunkers underneath the school. Still partially transfixed by the clouds outside, his teacher picked him up.

As they walked down the stairwell, the window to the side of them began to darken to a muddy brown colour, the ravaging dexterity of the clouds formation drawing ever closer. Descending the last few steps, her body twisted round into a small but measurable hollow, which was dug into the side of the wall, quickly she placed him down and took a stand next to his headmistress.

Each of the children looked startled and scared, but both of those emotions had escaped him and he was unsure why. For him, the colour of the clouds produced a different fear, a subdued fear. He had only been a few years old, but the day his mother had been taken in front of his eyes, as the Storm formed in the sky above him, he had felt the fear in his father's eyes . He had not been able to find reason for that in the skies above, aside from the large sodden brown clouds that hung there, motionless.

The screams filled his ears to this day. As he sat there with the murmuring filling the air around him, able to hear the wind beginning to pick up as doors banged in the hollow body of the school, he wondered if this storm might bestow the same type of killer hatred over them all, like some kind of wild animal. Suddenly, glass began to shatter around him, the frames waning under the roar of the wind outside.

A sudden smash on the steps. Instantly set the children ablaze, each screaming at the noise. The teachers were trying their best to quell the children's apparent shock, as pieces of glass and twisted metal fell down the marble steps and onto the dark and dusty bunker floor. His teacher immediately walked over to him as it fell.

"Graciou, what's wrong?" she said.

But he only stared into her eyes, for he knew that he did not fear the object, nor the circumstance, but he did not know why, for the fear was real to all around him. It was half his reason for searching the skies the way he did, as if waiting to see some sort of answer among the white rough clouds, but the answers never came. Even though they were so small, they felt so huge to him. She turned away making sure the other children were well, the ones that required her attention more than he did. Comforting them as best she could, the sound from the wind outside continuing to increase, as pieces of broken stone and twisted beams could be heard falling on the floors above.

Hours later the noise had subsided and there was a silence in the air around them. His headmistress stood and walked out onto the bunker floor, looking up toward the marble steps and the rest of the school. Slowly Graciou began to hear footsteps as her eyes watched invisible figures, moving down towards her.

"Miriam, are you all right?"

He heard from the steps above.

"Yes, I think so."

"What about the children?" he answered back.

"They're fine, just somewhat shook up."

Her voice was exasperated. There was a pause and then the voice spoke again.

"The damage is too extensive to carry on teaching for today. I'd recommend sending the children home."

She nodded in his direction, his form masked by the wall that jutted outward to the side of his view.

"I'll make sure the parents know to come and collect them."

Graciou watched her eyes as they looked up the marble steps towards whispered words, that Graciou could not hear. Nodding once more, she turned back to the children with an expression of relief.

"Children, pair up and follow me to the main hall."

Getting up from the bench, he slid off, planting his feet firmly in the dirt-ridden concrete. He watched, as each of the other children popped off the high, pew-like benches that flanked both sides of the bunker, each still scared and tired. Lost in thought, he found himself being picked up again by his teacher as she carried him up the marble steps and into the main corridor, passing by his classroom as she did so, glass now littering most of the floor.

A large and formidable boulder lay firm and rigid over the very section of classroom he had been sat in. Her eyes looked around as the rest of the children walked into the hall, but not before her eye caught a glimpse of the boulder. She rested for a second, staring at it, quickly whipping her gaze back toward Graciou who was still wondering what was happening. She brushed his hair from his fringe and continued to walk through to the main hallway.

The big large mahogany doors creaked open, large statues and moulded figures haunting the walls around them, as they had always done. The children sat at the stone bench in the middle of the room. The man that Graciou guessed had been speaking earlier, was standing just in front of it.

"I've notified all the parents..." He said, lowering his voice once more.

"His father's busy currently, but they say he'll be here as soon as possible."

He could see she was disheartened. For he knew that she was upset to see him waiting on his father, though he bore no sign of being bothered by it. His father's duties extended not just to his own kin, but also to that of everyone. Each of the children slowly filtered out of the room, leaving him alone with his headmistress, who was holding him to her, as if trying to cushion him from the silence and the waiting. Watching his feet, he pushed one foot forward and watched as the other fell back, then pushed the other forward and watched as it fell back. Passing the time was now something he found quite easy to do.

Hours later his father's figure hurried in holding one of the large entrance doors open, his large hands and predominant face met by his own. Instantly, he walked over to him, picking him up into his embrace.

"How's he been doing Miriam?"

"He's been fine, as always Excem."

He paused for a slight second, just enough for him to notice it.

"And how is the school?"

"Not too good, Marcus said there was extensive damage to most of the building."

"I will make sure I get men onto the building as soon as the morning comes. Thank you for looking after him." She smiled and looked into Graciou's eyes, giving his cheeks a small but affectionate stroke.

His father strode out of the hallway into the dust-filled street instantly masking what was around him, creating a cocoon inside of his massive sheepskin coat, shielding his mind from the destruction he did not know, with the stories of his day.

"So how was your day son?"

He didn't reply, not something he often did, but he was unable to understand what had happened and wished he knew how to speak of it.

"That good, hey! Well, I'm sure we can find something interesting when we get back home. Daddy's been very busy today, so many people to meet."

He gave him a small kiss on the head.

"Sorry I was so late picking you up. But they had a lot to talk about."

His father stopped again, his massive stride taking them ever closer to his home. Every now and again he could see a flurry of black cloth as he looked out over his father's shoulder. Even though the sheepskin coat hugged his body tightly, he could still peep out through the slit just under the back of his hat and he was sure that there had been movement.

"Here we are…"

He knew that they had reached the gate by the way his father's voice had changed, but something in his grip made him feel uneasy. Lifting him off his hip he placed him down amongst some broken pieces of stone.

"Do you remember when we played yesterday?"

"When we played dead Daddy?" Graciou said innocently.

"Yes, when we played dead. This is very important; I want you to do exactly what you did yesterday. Can you do that for Daddy?"

He nodded and shut his eyes fast, he could remember what they had been doing the day earlier. His father had told him to sit very still and shut his eyes closed. If he moved when something drew closer he got chastised for it, but if he remained motionless and still, against the grass, he was rewarded.

He had remembered that even when his father had drawn closer to him and tried to wake him, he had to stay still. For if he moved or opened his eyes he would be told off for doing so. Lying in between the cragged pieces of stone he listened to the sounds of the wind, just able to make out the sound of something flapping in the breeze above him.

But there had been nothing there to make such a noise. Nor had there been any flags, or other such objects that would behave that way close by. Then, steps shuffled across the ground around him, each appearing to come closer and then stop and then appear further away than they had before. It sounded like several people were tiptoeing around him, but he couldn't understand why.

He then heard a few vague but persistent short shots, which sounded much like his father's own rifle. Slowly, the steps stopped and he was able to hear nothing more than the sound of the wind once more around him, remaining still, until his father began to prod him. But even then he would-n't wake.

"Wake up Graciou," his father said affectionately.

But he stuck fast, keeping his eyes closed firmly. Until he heard the sound of his fathers laughter, which made him open them.

"You can wake up now…"

Opening one eye he looked up at him.

"Was that good Daddy?"

"Brilliant, even better than me."

Smiling he picked him up and strode over to the gates of his home, his father looking back at the pieces of broken rock and wood.

Inside, the castle was large and each of its rooms had small balconies that protruded out with good views of the gardens below. Each of the steps and sets of stairs were carved from the finest marble and each glistened in the late evening sun.

The pictures and paintings that were hung on each wall were of much amusement to his eyes. Pictures of great men stood with weapons by their sides, pictures of landscapes stretching out into the distance and pictures of scenes of retreat and scenes of victory. He knew what the scenes were but he knew not of where they were, or why they had occurred. For each held a story that his father knew only too well, but only a few had been explained to Graciou and they were of the men that stood in the pictures.

He remembered distinctly when he was four years old being told about the first of the pictures in the house. It was situated above the great stair-case just off from the opening to the front of the castle, a massive picture, at least the full size of the swirling staircase above it. The man stood proud in it with his blade by his side, unsheathed and dirty. His face reddened by a colour that his eyes had not yet seen, and his clothes were darkened with a darkness that his dreams had not yet shown him.

But the story contained within the frame of the picture and its strange apperance, was one he remembered throughout each and every glimpse of it. The man in the picture was that of his great, great, great grandfather, a man of stature and positive energy. He had stood at the tide of the great arm, which swept out toward the enemy that surrounded his men; he was wounded more mortally that day than any other. But even though he had been wounded badly by the fighting, his heart had continued to bear him through his years, before coming to meet his fate in death just before Graciou's birth.

His father placed his large hat down onto the chair and turned to the servant girl that had appeared at the head of the entrance.

"Good afternoon Mary. I trust you're feeling well?"

"Yes sir, though my mother and father have been working hard all day. There was extensive work to be done in the village."

His father nodded thoughtfully.

"I know, remember that if they ever require anything they have only to ask and the same of you as well." She smiled.

"Yes sir. Will you require anything?"

Turning to look down at him with an enquiring face, his father began to ask.

"Are you hungry Graciou?"

"Thirsty…"

"Just a drink of orange for the Master."

"Right you are."

She trailed off into a passage, behind the wall of the corridor, leaving him stood with his father. He was such a giant to his eyes. From the day he had been born he had appeared huge in front of him, his sword was always kept by his side, the same as that of his rifle, though that was always kept hidden from sight underneath his clothing. His dress complimented how he wanted to be seen in private as well as with the townspeople. Once, he heard his father say, that it best complimented the people around him and lowered his status to that of any other man, for those people were the most important to him, second of course to his son.

"Graciou?"

"Yes, Daddy?"

"I'll be in the study if you need me, but make sure you wait for Mary to come back with that drink and remember to be polite."

"I will Daddy."

His father walked off to the left, to his study, opening the doors before walking through them and out of eyesight. Heeding his father's words, he sat himself down in front of his father's study.

Mary soon walked back from the servant's passageways that ran behind the walls, with his drink in her hand.

"Is that all Master?" she said, placing the drink down onto the table, which was in front of him.

He nodded slowly, but she didn't retreat back to the kitchens and her duties. She had always taken a liking to him and ever since he had been tiny she had spoken to him when no-one else was around.

"So what did you do today hmm?"

"Nothing."

Her eyes came down to meet his, enquiring if there was any life at all inside them.

"Don't you want to go and find something to do?"

His face lit up a little and watching her take his hand in his, they both climbed up the steps past the large painting of his Grandfather. The castle was very quiet and he didn't see anyone else as they continued along the corridors to his room, entering to find that his play-chest was tidy and the room was free of any disruption. Instantly he went over to the chest, opened it and got out most of his favourite toys. Ever since his mother died it seemed he had spent more and more time with the girl, Mary.

She obviously enjoyed looking after him when no one else was around to do so. Behind him he could hear her working over the sheets and looking at his clothes in the wardrobe, stopping every so often to take out items from it and place them at the end of the bed. After she had finished she walked over to him, and sat down next to the myriad of toys that were filling the floor, starting to play with some of them with him. He had been fairly content, playing with the toys, but inside his mind the images of the day were still more present and he stopped playing as his eyes stared outward at the open balcony looking up into the dark murky sky.

"What do you see Graciou?" she said worriedly.

Staring for a second he pondered the cloud front, as Mary got up and walked over to the balcony, looking back at him apprehensively.

"It's clear," he said, as if it were not an issue.

Safe in what her eyes had shown her, she walked back over to him, sitting once more beside the chest.

"I saw a storm today."

Her eyes looked up and met with his, as if the conversation had taken a turn that she couldn't follow. She smiled and returned his gaze trying desperately not to answer the question he had already asked.

"Why did I see it before anyone else?"

Her eyes looked up again.

"I can't talk about it Graciou, it's forbidden."

He couldn't understand why they weren't allowed to talk about it, and it only grieved him more as he played with her and the hours drew on. Finally she got up, aware of the time.

"Look at the time, I need to go and make sure your dinner's ready. Can you tell your father it will be ready at the normal time?"

He nodded again and she knew that it was a yes. She had learned well to follow what he said by his body language, and it was not often he used fountains of speech to get his answer across. She left, closing the door behind her, the walls of the room beginning to illuminate, slowly adjusting to the darkness outside and inside the castle. He gave himself a few minutes with his toys, and then got up to find that time had accumulated into more than just minutes.

"Did Mary ask you to come and get me?" his father said at the doorway, with a tone of seriousness. He looked around for some words but couldn't think of what to say, his toys had taken priority over the matter.

"Never mind let's go and eat. Your Uncle Harass and Barnabe are back, they've been out hunting all day long."

His eyes met the dining room as they both went in and sat down at the table, his father heading the table, with his uncles sat down the right hand side and a chair drawn up for him at the opposite side.

"GRACIOU!"

He knew instantly who it was as he entered the room. Harass had bellowed forth and his father had taken a step backward and then re-adjusted himself, gently pushing him forward.

"Uncle Harrass, how was your hunting trip?"

"Hunt…Ooh…Yes it was most brilliant; we caught a few deer. Even managed to catch ourselves a few wild birds too."

His smile was positive, and his shaggy but clean beard appeared to illuminate his jolly nature.

"Shame the birds weren't chirping in the trees by the time we got there."

His other uncle Barnabe appeared to direct the comment at the starter that met his face in front of him.

"Well, let's get you sat down Graciou."

His father lifted him up into the chair and they each began to sip the soup that was in front of them.

"Did you send those letters away Excem?"

"Yes, I sent them earlier. I should guess they will reach the residence by the early morning."

The conversation appeared alien to him and he couldn't understand quite why they weren't speaking as they usually did. It was as if a fog of mystery had descended over them. Neither spoke of the weather, and his Uncle Barnabe continued to stare at his soup as the bowl was slowly and yet steadily drained.

"Wine, Harass?" The head servant said, walking over to him.

"Please, just a touch."

"Sir?" he said to his father.

"I'm fine, thank you."

"And what would you like Master?"

The head servant, the father of Mary, was standing by the table looking down at him.

"Orange, please."

"Right you are master."

He took a pause as he often did, waiting to see if that was all, and then ended by leaving the room closing the doors behind him. Graciou's mind still continued to run around in circles with the image of the Storm he had seen earlier, for he had never actually seen a storm build before and not with such ferocity. He was pulled in by it; his mind couldn't let the image leave, it clung there daring him to enquire about it and finally he burst.

"I saw a storm today."

His words filled the already silent room as the head servant entered with the drinks, pausing for a second and then continuing.

"I knew it!" Barnabe half shouted across the table.

"Hush, Barnabe!" his father had interjected quickly as if trying to stifle whatever it was he was going to say, but getting up, Barnabe was obviously not in favour of his father's interjection.

"Enough for me I think. I shall depart to my room for the evening. Enjoy your meal Gentlemen."

His Uncle got up, leaving Harrass and his father still a little bemused with what he had said, wine being poured slowly into the glasses. Harrass gave his father an overseeing look, as if asking his permission for something. He appeared to get it as he spoke.

"What did you see Graciou?" he said, pensively.

"I was watching the clouds form on the horizon. I could see the clouds billowing and then they changed from white to brown."

He looked up at his Uncle Harrass looking for some sort of answer.

"Did you see anything else, Graciou?"

His father's words were cold, but they seemed to be steeped with a sense of deep sincerity, as if he was trying to protect him from something.

"A piece of rock flew out of the cloud, then I began to see more of them. Each rock came closer and closer to the school."

His father's fist hit the table with a heavy thud, instantly making his wine splash out across it. He'd never seen his father act in anger before and he couldn't understand what was making them all so on edge.

"We've got to tell him Excem. We can't..." said Harrass quickly, but what did they need to tell him?

"We have to protect him from what he cannot see."

"He's seen it Excem, we can't protect him from what he's seen!"

"Listen to me Harrass! We are NOT telling him anything!"

"One of these days Excem he will wonder what exactly happened and our pursed lips will be the…"

Harrass stopped and looked toward Graciou, then back at his father.

"The undoing of this family!"

But his father was decisive and answered back quickly.

"No I cannot, I will not."

"No and I know that you won't."

His Uncle got up from the table nodding to the head servant who was by the wall. He didn't appear to venture any closer.

"Daddy, did I say something wrong?"

"No Graciou, no, you didn't do anything."

That night his dreams were filled with the clouds billowing and jutting forward in front of him, each cloud bringing a new and ever present danger closer. But what danger was it he thought he felt? What was so close that his father wouldn't even speak of it?

He knew not the reason why, and for the rest of the night his sleep was met with images of the cloud formations, rising and falling on the horizon like waves upon the sea.

He woke the next morning to find the castle quiet and filled with the smell of food rising up from the kitchens. Mary was already waiting in the room beside his bed.

"Did you sleep well Graciou?" she said as he began to wake.

"I had nightmares."

"What about?"

"About the storm I saw yesterday."

She had been tugging his shirt over his head, but stopped, then proceeded knowing she had to say something.

"I'm sure they will go away Graciou. It's probably just another bad dream."

He didn't force it, for he knew that she was still not able to speak truly of what he had seen. Walking him down and into the dining room, she put him into the chair next to his father and walked away.

"Good morning, Graciou."

His father's voice sounded tired and heavy, as if he was restless.

"How is the repair work coming along?" his father said to the head servant, who had been waiting by the table.

"It's coming along well sir, most of the buildings are being rebuilt as we speak."

"Good, I think I will assist with the process later, after I have heard back from Harrass."

He nodded and walked out of the room; his father turned to him at this point.

"So then, what do you think we should do?"

His father smiled and he thought for a minute of what would be fun, but his mind was soon broken by the sound of Mary in the corridor sounding worried. His father looked away, frowning in the direction of the south-facing door.

His Uncle Harrass entered the room; his face was marred with gashes and cuts.

"Harrass! What the hell happened?"

But Harass didn't answer. His face was pale and he dropped at the foot of the door, his father and the head servant instantly rushing over to his side.

"HARRASS!" his father roared as he shook his shoulders, but no matter how much he tried he would not wake.

Out of his two uncles Graciou's Uncle Harrass was the one he had felt the closest too. But he couldn't understand why his father was crying so much. Sliding down from the chair, he walked over to the stiff body of Harrass and threw his arms around his father's neck, trying to understand why he was crying.

"He's gone, Sir..."

The servants voice breached the silence that had filled the room, and he unclenched his father's hands from Harrass' coat. His father turned to him and gave him a large hug then unlinked his arms from his neck.

"Mary can you..." he said, as she walked in.

"Of course Sir."

Mary came over and picked him up from his father's grip, but his hand was weak and fell away all too easily.

"Mary..." his father said, as she was walking out of the room.

"Sir?"

"If he talks to you, let him talk."

Nodding, she left the room, walking up the steps towards his room, leaving the distant shouting of his father's voice shooting out from the corridors and rooms on the bottom floor.

As they walked into his room she set him down on the bed, sitting next to him, apparently less emotional than his father, but still affected by what had happened.

"Why was Daddy crying?"

"Because your uncle had a hunting accident," she said, her voice pierced with sadness.

"How do you know?"

"Because I saw him come in, he was wheezing badly, he told me to go and get some help quickly. But I could see it was a shooting wound that had done it."

What she had said made sense, but why his uncle would have been so careless, or another so careless with him, he could not understand. Why had he appeared at the doorway of their dining room, bleeding from the mouth with cuts to his face? Even if he had been shot why did he look as if he had been thrown through a wall in the process?

Suddenly, they both heard a loud bang from somewhere downstairs in the castle, Mary instantly turned around in front of him, as if masking him from something that was not even there.

"Graciou! Get under the bed quickly."

He did as she asked, swiftly he got underneath it, she soon followed and both of them lay on the floor trying to keep as quiet as possible. Then he began to hear unannounced footsteps in the room. Mary quickly covered his mouth, making sure he did not make a single sound. He could just see feet underneath the rim of the bed as they moved from the balcony toward the doorway of his bedroom. But as they did, another set of feet appeared to be moving in quite a different direction.

Something was next to his head just inches from him on the other side of the bed, obviously looking for signs of them. He could see soundless tears running off her face now, as she stared at the place where the sound was issuing from, continuing to hold his mouth firmly from making a sound. The footsteps started to move away from him but still persisted to stay near the bedside, then the movement stopped and he thought for a second he could hear the faint rustling of sheets. He had been right however, for he saw the sheets lifted on Mary's side, opening the gap underneath the bed to let light flood in from the balcony behind.

"HELP!"

He heard her voice scream out, penetrating past his eyes and ears to anyone who was close enough to come and save them both. The figure was kneeling just below the sheets of the bed but as soon as it had heard her, a hand had been thrown underneath to grab at her dress. She quickly fought back trying to hurt the man who was now grabbing for her.

Then a sound from the doorway issued their relief; he could hear a hissing sound as something flew through the air, the man's grip falling instantly silent. Moving forward she tried to see what had stopped the man from moving.

"Hello?" she said, to whoever might be there.

"Mary? Is that you?"

"Thank God, yes it's me, I'm under the bed."

A face appeared, it was the face of his other Uncle Barnabe, he looked worn and his eyes looked even more worn, as if the night hadn't been one of any great sleep for him either.

"Graciou's in here too?"

"Yes, I took him after Harrass entered the dining room."

"Is Harrass all right?"

He helped them both out from under the bed, Barnabe's face becoming pale.

"Didn't you see him?"

"No, what happened?"

She paused but not for too long, as it appeared time was not on their side.

"He walked into the castle as I was moving from the dining room. He was really badly hurt, I called for the doctor straight away…but it was too late."

A silent emotion covered his face, as if he were, in the few seconds he had, trying to grieve for a person he loved and yet had always hidden that love from. Throwing his arms forward he picked up Graciou. He couldn't ever remember being picked up by him before, it appeared that whatever was happening was not as his mind had portrayed it.

"Come on we've got to get out of here quickly."

But before either of them had reached the doorway, he had been met with yet another man, if the person could be called that. Graciou fled from his Uncle's hands, as the dark pitted face of whatever it was leered at them from just outside of the doorway. Without hesitation his Uncle flew out of the doorway and into the man, knocking him from sight, several gunshots issuing from somewhere outside. Mary instantly came over to him clasping his head close to her body.

"Are you all right Barnabe?" she said, toward the silent doorway.

"I'll be all right, take Graciou out of the castle. Head for the secret passage."

She appeared to dither for a second with fear, numbed by the events that had taken place.

"HURRY girl!"

Picking him up in her arms, she began running out of the doorway to find Barnabe half impaled on the brickwork that overhung onto the staircase. Some short arms fire instantly hit the bricks behind her head, and she ducked quickly to miss it. As he looked back, another few short shots from his uncle's commandeered weapon took out the person who had fired upon them. Their faces were so alien and strange; each of them appeared marred with a blackness that was beyond redemption. Their faces looked as if they had been painted.

Mary's feet skidded across the stone floors as she ran into the secret passageway, which spiralled downward. Running forward she picked up the torch that was lying at the top of the stairwell and carried on down. The staircase was long and it took forever for them to reach the base, but by the time they were there he could already hear the shouts of men outside. Light began to spill in from all sides as Mary continued to run with him still in her arms, the low sun blinding her slightly as she ran. Behind him he could see the opening, which had been masked by shrubs and trees. From the sky above him he could see black shimmers descending down onto the roof of the castle and when seeing him, they turned their guns toward them.

"Mary over here!"

From somewhere up ahead Barnabe's voice had issued and continuing to run forward, she eventually found him, lying behind a makeshift barrier of wooden boxes.

"Barnabe, what the…?"

But he quickly stopped her from asking any questions.

"Not enough time girl, we've got to get Graciou out of here."

"Where are my mother and father?" she said, steadily becoming more and more exasperated.

"We don't know, we've been cut off from the rest of the castle."

He was placed down onto the grass just behind the makeshift barrier, which blocked the gunfire to an adequate degree.

"What's going on Barnabe?"

"I have no idea, but right now our number one priority is Graciou."

He heard his name again, and he could see that it was for good reason. Barnabe was bleeding from his right leg, where a large wound had opened up in his knee, badly masked with a piece of cloth. The situation was not looking too good for any of them where they currently were and the gunfire had grown more intense. Mary had already fallen back down to him, trying to shield him from the unknown, which appeared at this moment to be everywhere.

"Where can we go?"

A shot signalled from behind them and Barnabe instantly fell backward, his right shoulder bleeding profusely from the shot.

"BARNABE!"

Mary cried out, as one of the men who was kneeling next to him turned to see what was wrong.

"Sir, are you all right?"

The man said quickly.

"I'll be fine."

But the wound was deep and Barnabe was beginning to look pale.

"Let me get the wound for you," Mary said, and even though her intention was good, she would have been putting herself in danger to walk or even crawl forward at this current moment.

"Don't worry about me Mary, I'll keep. Just make sure you watch Graciou."

She heard his words, which were heavily decisive and returned to Graciou. He was now beginning to wonder what was happening around him, and inside his eyes and heart he began to feel a void opening up.

"We've got to get these two out of here," said the man beside them.

Barnabe turned round looking down the thin line, which was their front, as he said.

"Marcus, get over here!" Barnabe shouted. The same man who had been in his school the day before could be seen running toward them. He found it strange that he was also here now.

Marcus came running under the small wooden entrance to the storehouse and hit the ground, smiling at him for a minute, as if he had never seen him.

"We've got to get these two out of here Captain."

He noticed them exchange a glance that appeared to mean something more than his words, but what they were saying he was quite unsure of.

"I understand Sir."

He turned, looking in Mary's direction as he did so.

"What's your name Madam?"

"Mary…" she said weakly.

"Follow me Mary, don't be scared, we'll get you both out of here."

Marcus got up from the ground and issued a command to the rest.

"Covering fire!"

He signalled to them both to move forward, and got up instantly as Mary threw her weight forward, hurrying to pick Graciou up. Within minutes they were walking through the vegetation at the back of the garden, following a small dirt path.

"Through here, Mary."

Up ahead, he had passed through a short opening in one of the wooden walls that was built at the edge of the grounds. Through this the land opened out into a bleak and deserted tundra, filled with dunes.

"From here on in I need both of you to keep in contact with me, make sure you keep talking, it's easy to get lost."

As they followed him into the dunes, with the Storm all around them, he found it strange that it was not blowing them over, for he was sure it had the capability.

"Where are we going Marcus?" she said, with an edge of apprehension, about their destination.

"I don't know yet, but I know there's a village not far from here, I just hope we can reach it in time." He paused; his tone changed to one of worry and he carried on. "Barnabe said he had no idea what was happening back at the castle. I heard something happened to Harrass?"

He instantly remembered Harrass's face as he had entered the dining hall, and his father's face turning from a carefree smile to that of a much more pressing anxiety.

"From what I hear he came into the dining hall," said Marcus, appearing to hurry her for an answer.

"I was there when it happened Marcus, but what was he doing?"

"I've asked all the men, but they say that his mission was held and kept. They know not of what he was doing or why he was doing it. All they know is that the mission wasn't heading into unfriendly territory. There's no reason for him to have been hurt so badly. It makes no sense, no sense at all," she said.

"Indeed it doesn't and I cannot begin to fathom what has," he stopped dead in his speech, looking blankly into Graciou's eyes, as if he were apprehensive of saying something in his presence.

"I'm thirsty Mary," he said, as their walk began to draw on, for it felt like they had been walking for hours.

"We'll get you a drink soon don't worry Graciou."

He kept himself quiet while the sand continued to whip at his face, turning forward from Mary's arms, every few minutes to see if there was any sign of life ahead. The dunes continued to roll and looked completely endless and dead. Just as he had started to fall asleep in her arms, their view changed ahead, a rocky outcrop appeared to part, it's entrance still masked by the dust of the Storm.

"Is this the village Marcus?" Mary said with anxiety in her voice.

Marcus had now walked out of sight, and neither himself nor Mary could see him. They both continued to walk, each step drawing them closer and closer into the narrow corridor, which appeared to cut through the rocks. Ahead of them a coach was waiting, with a large collection of boxes and cases at the rear.

"Marcus?"

Her voice filled the silent air without response, and then from somewhere up ahead his voice echoed. She appeared to loosen her grip on him and relax slightly.

"You know what to do?" his voice said indirectly, as they began to see a dark outline in front of them.

"What's going on Marcus?"

"It's all right Mary…"

"No it's not all right, what's going on?"

Marcus stepped forward, with another man by his side.

"I'm not supposed to say, but seeing as you're likely to get yourself hurt if I don't…" he paused, thinking she might not press the issue.

"Yes?" she said sternly.

"Ever since we were told to guard Graciou, we've been part of a pact between ourselves and his father. That pact has a section devoted to that of him only. It states that if something were to happen and his father could not be consulted that I was to bring him here."

"What pact? I've never…"

Her eyes narrowed as she kept her distance from him.

"I cannot say more than that, if I do I will be breaking my oath pledged to his father."

"Stuff the damn pledge Marcus! Tell me what's going on here."

Her voice was trembling and he knew she couldn't trust his word, for all it's worth, she needed the proof to understand what was happening.

"Graciou is all that's important now, the coach man here will take you to a safe place."

"Hang on Marcus, why…?"

Marcus smiled at her, as he passed by, toward the edge of the opening.

"There are other clauses in that pact, that stretch beyond the birth of Graciou, to that of yourself Mary."

She stopped, still unable to understand what was being said, Marcus reassured her once more, saying:

"You've got to trust me on this. Make sure that Graciou grows up knowing nothing but what he already knows. Keep him safe…"

The last few words, were said as if he were guilt ridden, it was like he disagreed with what he was doing. Suddenly gunshots flared into the opening from behind, instantly ricocheting off the hard stone walls, and Marcus threw his hands out to grab Graciou and place him into the coach.

"GET IN MARY!"

His voice was loud and clear in the air and the firing became more persistent as his voice died. Marcus fell away from the window, as the coach began to pull away, gunfire pummelling his body. The carriage drew round the bend through the dim mist. Where to? Graciou did not know.

2

It was fourteen years to the day since those events had taken place around him, and he still did not understand what had happened. His mind was just able to recollect the few images of what had occurred: his uncle falling at the opening to one of the rooms in his father's house, their escape from the attackers, and that of Marcus.

His life was different now, both in his environment and the way in which Mary had come to see it. They had been dropped off at a small house at the edge of open woodland, quickly having to settle down into their new lives. Graciou had learnt to ride and one of the men from the town had shown him how to put a weapon to good use; he was already the best among his peers and outshone the best fighters in the village. A trait which he always wondered came because of his past.

Mary had taken over as his guardian, as if she had been nurturing him most of his life. But over the years things had changed and Graciou had begun to notice her eyes fading as the days had drawn on, each night bringing a new and ever more present stare to them.

He was now in his eighteenth year and was fast approaching his inauguration ceremony as a sign of coming of age. It entailed various small tasks that he needed to complete, as well as a speech in front of the village public.

"You look a little anxious?" his eyes lifted slowly from the soup that lay in front of him, Mary's words piercing his thoughts.

"I'm just thinking about the ceremony."

He smiled, continuing to fondle the soup with his spoon. She returned the look on his own face, but he knew she wouldn't talk about what had become of the past, of the memories, faded to old grey, like dark books lining a shelf.

"Do you remember that day Mary?"

Her eyes looked up, he had barely talked about it and the very idea of it had passed long before this day, in his mind. But now it seemed to be communicating with him in a way that he had not felt before, like a deep longing inside him, to understand his past.

"Which day?"

He knew she was hiding, but he felt it high time they began to talk about it.

"I'm not a kid anymore," he said sternly.

"You remember what Marcus said that day?" he said continuing.

"Nearly to the letter, why must we speak about it?"

"I just wish I knew what had happened to them, I wish I knew what all this meant."

"All this?" she said, enquiring about it.

"We've been here for fourteen years now Mary, doesn't it even cross your mind, why we were hurried away from all of it so quickly?"

"Well, I thought it was because our lives were in danger."

Her voice had grown a little too care-free for him, he still felt that there was something more to it than she had ever suggested.

A knock at the door behind them, made them both jump, each turning in their chairs, Mary quick to return to her food as she spoke, as if no such reaction had taken place.

"Come in, it's not locked."

The door swung open and in stepped the proud face of his teacher. Since he had been roughly fifteen and Mary had let him go and train with William and the other village folk, he had been learning the art of fighting and hunting.

"Hi Mary, how are you both?"

"We're good Will."

She smiled pleasantly but she continued to leave the rest of the conversation to them alone. William turned to greet him, instantly looking all the more enthusiastic, though Graciou as unsure why.

"So how's the speech coming along?"

Graciou stared blankly round the room as if searching for some sort of answer.

"I'd offer to help if you need it." Will said.

"Wouldn't go amiss, I can't remember the last time I had so much difficulty writing something like this."

Graciou opened the drawer underneath the table and pulled out a piece of worn paper and a pencil.

"This is all I've got so far."

The paper showed four sentences each marked by several scribbles and inconsistent patches among the words.

"Well let's see…"

Mary got up from the table clearing away the unfinished soup and returning to the duties of the house. They both went over the speech he had already began to write out on paper. By the time they had finished a cool breeze had begun to move amongst the rest of the house and the Will had managed to rectify most of the weaker areas.

"I think that's worthy of any public ceremony, those big words should make it look fancy too. You know the village folk, hard of hearing and all that."

Will gave him a nod and continued to put on his coat and hat.

"I'll be off now Mary, good luck for the ceremony Graciou."

"Nice to see you Will."

Graciou smiled as he left the doorway and Mary's eyes met his as she sat down at the table.

"Better?" she said.

"Much better, just needed a bit of help with what I wanted to say." She smiled.

"Good, well I think I shall go off to bed. You can do as you want for a while. But don't forget about the ceremony tomorrow."

She stepped up from the table, leaving him to his piece of paper and the nervous flurries that had entered his stomach. He placed the paper down onto the table softly and rubbed his eyes, looking up toward the ceiling where the kerosene lamp was lit. Lifting a hand to the lamp he slowly turned the brass handle, as each shade of bronze orange softly dimmed, leaving the house quiet and still.

His eyes quickly moved to the only window that was open, the dark blue sky above showing no threat of rain or cloud. His mind was all too quick to remember the darkness that he had seen upon the horizon that day so many years ago, and the thought would not leave him as the night lingered on.

3

Graciou woke from his sleep late in the day rubbing his head as he woke. The paper was still on the table as it had been from the night before and he was instantly reminded of where he should probably already be. Picking up the paper and putting on some of his more formal clothes, he shut the door of the house and started walking through the woods toward the village.

The house was situated just down from the village, on the very edge of the forest, and had kept them warm and dry through the many winter months. It was now summer and the heat was a welcome one, forest trees hung like needles around him as he passed through the forest, noting as he always did, the ghostly feeling within the wood. Each tree looked as dead as the next, and as a child he'd got lost more than once just trying to get from the village to his home. As he drew closer he could see that the village was full of banter and joyous occasion, it appeared that the party had already begun. He smiled, able to see Will already with a cup in hand, soon sighting him coming out of the woods and separating the masses for his arrival.

"GRACIOU!" he bellowed as he came across, obviously already half drunk as it was.

The village people often got drunk at times of great celebration, for the rest of their days were filled with hard labour and work. When they got a chance to enjoy themselves, they really did and Graciou had always enjoyed the atmosphere, their lives were behind closed doors, much harder than they appeared, but they were good people. People in the crowd gradually started to come across to him, asking him how he was and how the trials had been, and his younger friends were mostly over in the corner of the congregation forming there own small area in which to watch the proceedings.

"Sorry I'm a bit late Will."

"Not to worry. We're ready when you are anyway. Just don't make it too late or people won't have any idea what those big words mean."

Will gave a look of terror at the thought and returned to a large stall behind him, which seemed to be carrying food of various varities.

Dominic Took

The event had been situated at the far end of the village in an open field, where it was events like these usually took place. Graciou began to walk over to the others, where he sat himself down on one of the wooden crates.

"Hey Graciou, how you doing?"

It was one of his closest friends and yet strangely he still felt no great affinity towards him, as if somehow he was distanced, though he had never understood why that was.

"Pretty good Tom, thanks for asking."

"No drink I see?" Tom was quick to ask and Graciou wasn't surprised, why was it the case he always had to have a drink in his hand?

"Not if I want to get this one out in one go," he said quickly.

"Sure, it'd calm your nerves you know."

"Sure it would, but not quite yet, hey."

"Suit yourself."

Each of them returned to their drinks and he began to survey the crowd, knowing that as soon as he felt it was right he could walk up onto the stand and get their attention.

"So when are you thinking of going up?" Tom said out of the corner of his eye.

"No time like the present I guess."

"Good luck then."

"Thanks."

Getting up, he walked through the crowd as he slowly started to climb the steps of the stand and walk to the centre of it. His chest felt tight and his stomach felt as if it were being stirred by some massive spoon. But the feeling soon left him as he saw a face he had not expect to see, coming out of the woods. It was Mary, she was stood away from the crowd, but just close enough to see and hear him.

He took the piece of paper out of his pocket and looked at the words, wishing they had meant more when he had written them, or rather Will had written them.

"Attention everyone! The boy wants to say something."

From the crowd one of the men had put a stopper in their talking and he was left pausing as he looked down at the first sentence of his paper.

"Firstly I'd like to thank you all for coming."

The crowd continued to be silent waiting for his speech to unravel.

"Though the transition into the community here hasn't been a quick one, I feel now, that I am more at home here than ever I have been. This is…"

His voice trailed off as he looked out into the woods; something was moving among them that no one else had seen. Something dark and hooded, something that looked most unfriendly. With an automatic feeling of danger his body moved, as he dropped from the stage trying to follow it with his eyes, Will and Mary noticing his apparent change in character coming toward him to find out what was wrong. The crowd stifled as he tried to break them apart, looking for the figure somewhere over them, but even though his height gave him some advantages he could not see it, anywhere he looked.

"Graciou what's wrong?" Will asked.

The figure continued to move and he did not stop as the crowd began to part a way for him.

"What's the matter?" Mary said coming toward him, as he finally broke free of the crowd, able to see the hooded figure turn behind the adjacent cottage and out of sight. Whatever it was had disappeared completely, but from where he had been standing it wanted to be seen.

"Graciou what's wrong?"

"Did you…"

He carried on walking, away from the crowd, to the back of the cottage. Where he now hoped to see whatever it was standing there. However instead he did not, whatever it was had vanished completely.

"Did I what Graciou?"

"Gra what's up?"

His friend had turned the corner to find him standing in the same spot, gaze still fixed upon the pathway looking for something.

"Its nothing; I thought, no, never mind."

Turning back, he walked to the stand, trying to recollect his thoughts and his speech as he went. But still unable to understand what he had seen, or what it had been and why he had even reacted like he had. But the feeling had been automatic, he had no control whatsoever when it happned.

As he finished the last line of his speech and the crowd applauded with a muted sense of enthusiasm, he tried to refocus his mind on what had happned, only to realise he had no way of understanding it. There was no cause for it to appear, none whatsoever. But he knew what he had seen and it was as real as anything.

Will walked onto the stage as he finished and presented him with his hunting sword, looking all the more concerned that he was all right. He smiled, indicating that he was fine. Deciding that it must have been nerves, but in his mind knowing that it must have been more he tried to force it out of his mind, continuing to drink for the rest of the night until he was more than relaxed. Returning home with his sword he found Mary at the table waiting.

"What happened out there earlier?"

He looked up trying to curb the reply, trying not to talk about it.

"Oh it was nothing."

"In all the years I've looked after you, I've never seen you make such a commotion as you did earlier."

"I saw something…some man."

"Just a man?"

"He was cloaked in black. I wanted to make sure that he wasn't trying to harm anyone."

His heart was still racing slightly, as his mind began to wonder whether he was becoming delusional.

"And you saw him go behind the cottage?"

"He walked in plain view of everyone, but no one else saw him, just me."

Her face looked worried as if he had taken some strange turn.

"You can't have seen anything else Graciou. Before you started running I thought I felt something behind me, but I glanced back and there was nothing there."

"Then why did you glance back?"

Her face looked strained as if she'd been meaning not to be so blunt about it.

"I don't know, but I didn't see a thing."

"I know what I saw and I don't understand why I saw it. Isn't it enough that you trust me?"

"I've trusted many people all my life Graciou, more you than any other and what I see is that all of you in time are no better than each other."

His eyes narrowed, as she turned standing up as she started to walk away from the table.

"What the hell is that supposed to mean?"

Opening the doorway she walked into her room locking the latch behind. He didn't bother to follow it up, as she was plainly not going to talk freely that evening. His mind was clouded with dead memories and unsleeping ghosts. Heavy with the scent of unknowing and a desperate need to understand what had taken place.

His mind awoke still sat at the chair of the table, the kerosene lamp's flame out above him. The shutters of each window were drawn and the doorway closed. It was still night, his eyes flicked around the room, surveying the pitch blackness. For some reason he felt as if the room wasn't quite as it seemed.

"Graciou?" The voice was elegantly etched with immovable anxiety and a sense that the person had been through more than their fair share of ordeals.

"How do you know my name, stranger?"

His voice permeated the air, his strength still intact inside.

"It's good to know you're still alive."

"Why wouldn't I be?"

"Don't you know who I am?"

He searched through his mind trying to figure out who it was. What did the voice sound like in the darkness?

"Don't you remember the gunfire?"

His mind fell upon the image of Marcus and somehow the image stood out to him..

"Marcus?"

"I've not come under that name for a great deal of time, but it was mine to hold once."

"Marcus is that really you?"

But he knew that it couldn't have been, for Marcus' dead and long since forgotten body was lying at the opening to the rocky outcrop they had once left so quickly.

"I don't have much time Graciou."

"I thought you were dead."

"Not dead, but I came very close to it. I've done so much to so many Graciou."

"What's happened to you Marcus?"

"What has consumed me is nearly done with the last dregs of strength that I have left."

He paused, taking what seemed to be short breaths through into his wheezing lungs.

"I come about…"

He stopped coughing and spluttering up what sounded like some sort of liquid. Again taking in masses of air as he stopped.

"Your father…"

His mind spun as he heard the words repeated again and again, it had been so long since he had heard of him that his mind had made him all but dead.

"What about my father?!" he exclaimed.

"AHH!"

Marcus cried out somewhere in front of him. Desperate to see what it was that had made the noise, he picked up his blade, igniting the kerosene lamp above the table to find a twisted and mangled form by the door in front of him, which had long since stopped resembling anything like Marcus.

"What the hell happened to you?!"

"Kill me now! Kill me before it takes me over completely! KILL ME GRACIOU!"

But in his mind his conflictions ran riot, if this truly was Marcus then why should he put his blade through him, he knew he was long since dead and had been for a very long time indeed. But this wasn't Marcus, whoever he had been or was, this was not him. Even if the memory had failed him, he could remember what he had done for them.

"If you don't kill me it will find you, i can't stop it, not anymore. Ahh!"

Graciou knew what he referred to, he knew exactly what Marcus meant and knew that the pain he was feeling could not have been without purpose.

"Forgive me Marcus."

His voice permeated with grief and forgiveness as he began to unsheathe his blade and extend his arm high above himself for the merciful blow. The form in front of him now changing giving him seconds upon which to hesitate with his attack, but its form was one that had plagued his memory for too long and he could take no more of it.

Beginning to change, its head became grossly elongated and its face changed to a blacked out mass, its black cloak enhancing the images that had long since been buried in his mind, its rifle illuminating even the most deadliest of ghosts from rising once more out of his dreams.

"AHH!"

It screamed, piercing the very walls of the cottage. Picking up the blade he raised it into the air above the mangled body, strengthening his grip as he plunged it down into what should have been Marcus below. Just as the last few breaths were crawling from its lungs, he noticed the creature's hand moving towards its chest and clutching underneath its rag for a shirt, at some unknown object. He continued to watch the creature as it's form metamorphosised and changed into something more human like.

"GRACIOU!" Mary's voice screamed from behind him.

His hunting blade dripping with blood and that of the morphed form returning to what it once was. Marcus's eyes dimly lit against the light, his blue pupils darkening against that of the white of his eyes.

"Graciou what..."

Coming back from the realisation of his actions he looked down at the soaked blade, trying to figure out what had truly just happened. Falling back against the table he continued to let his mind recoil at the action he had just taken, for no one now would believe what had just happened. Shocked, Mary stepped forward, trying to understand what it was.

"Oh God no, God no. How can it be?"

"I don't know, he appeared in the room...started talking about my father."

"What?" she said shocked.

"But why did you kill him?"

"I didn't kill him Mary, it wasn't him any more."

"If you're telling me that that is not Marcus, your eyes are blinded by the truth."

"Mary what's going on? Graciou are you all right!?"

From outside he began to hear shouting and it was obvious some of the villagers had heard something.

"They're going to catch me, they're going to take my blade away, everything I've ever wanted here."

"Wait, it won't come to that..."

She quickly said, but he knew what would come.

"There's no time, the entire village will be on this house soon and none of them will believe a thing you or I say."

"Then what can we do?"

What had been left of Marcus had only been true to a certain point, but he did feel as if his father must have been brought up for some reason. There was reason for his visit, to free himself of the demon that plagued him or to make him aware of some kind of danger. Whatever it was he knew which was the more likely.

"There is nothing more I can do here. Marcus came for a reason, he came as himself for a moment," Graciou paused, wondering how he could explain it to her. "That's not how he appears now I know, but if I don't go now, I'll just keep on wishing I'd known what his words meant."

There was another bang at the door.

"There are so many un-answered questions, they're starting to build up and press on my mind. I can't board them up any longer."

"No, there has to be another way," Mary said desperately.

From the door there was another series of loud bangs, it was obvious the scream of its death had been heard from the village.

"There's no time Mary, make a good life for yourself here, from now on I am handing over responsibility of me to myself. No longer will you have to worry where I am or if I'm safe."

Her eyes began to well as if a great weight had begun to lift from them, but that great weight had a torrent of emotion that came with it.

"Don't be sad, these years we've been here have been for a reason, but now I must find out my past."

He turned to Marcus's dead body, pulling apart his partially blood soaked shirt and looked at the article that was underneath. Graciou quickly bundling it into the pocket of his garments, lifted himself out of the window, closing one of the shutters slightly ajar behind him, so he could hear what might ensue.

Will's voice could soon be heard, instantly trying to comfort Mary.

"Oh Jesus, what happened?!" he shouted.

"Will, thank God, I don't know, I came in here and it was there."

She had shielded him once more by lying and he was sure now that his departure would allow her to live without fear of what might be comming after them both. As he descended into the night and it's unforeseen dangers. He looked back on his home for one more time before running through the heavy mist towards, he hoped, his home.

4

He woke the next day on the edge of a small outcrop. His eyes burned as he opened them, his entire body ached from the hard ground; he still hadn't eaten since days previous, but he was sure he could go without for a while yet. He had collapsed in the early hours of the morning, exhausted and in need of rest; half worried that Will would catch up with him and take him back. His bow and blade were still by him and he picked each up, stowing them securely across his back, before changing into some warmer clothes for his immediate journey ahead.

The air had long since cleared, and after he had packed away what he would need for his walk, he picked up the symbol he had found upon Marcus' body. He placed it over his head tucking the symbol to his chest for whatever protection it might give. It had been the cross of the Prophets and he could remember that his father would never take it off.

With his mind set, he began walking around the outskirts of the wood, making sure he checked for any prowlers or people that might be waiting to take him back to the village, but he found none as he walked. The rest of the morning running into late afternoon was sunny and calm, and the long grass whipped against his legs as he walked through it toward a perfect horizon, hopeful that some landmark would soon fill his gaze.

But as late evening commenced down upon him, no such landmark could be seen and he sat in the tall green grass taking off the top layer of clothes he had on, and in doing so watching the symbol fall out from over his chest garment. The back of the symbol showed something quite different to that of just a symbol, for it was encrusted with a circular object that kept four points, each pointing perpendicular to the next and holding themselves firmly underneath the glass. A red line had been gouged along the side and seemed to point toward something, but the line was not clean and didn't look as if a master craftsman had done it. He hesitated, wondering if what he now held was little less than some sort of deceit, reeling him in closer to that of the maker.

But with no other light to guide him he had only that to go on, and as he looked at it closer he could see small etched writing into that of the wood, which repeated the words "Gracious, Gracious, Gracious" three times across the wood, as if reciting a chant. It was so unnervingly close to his own name he began to wonder what exactly it was he had now taken onto his person. Why would a word so close to his own have been produced on such an item? His eyes escaped it, looking in the direction of the red point, scanning back and forth as the dark and transparent purples of the late evening sky began to elongate along their stretched form, arching away already from him, in the direction of the path he had taken.

Picking himself up, he held the object out, checking it every so often to make sure that the direction was correct, and that he had not in some way been deceived by it. But it appeared to remain consistent as the evening continued on. The red point which had appeared to have been pointing in the same direction, had slowly begun to arc round as if it were pointing toward something else. Following it he kept matching the two lines to check they were not pointing in erratic directions.

Underneath him he could feel his shoes slipping and rubbing against small granules of sand. He had managed to walk onto some sort of desert dune, so fixed on the artifact and its movements that he had not even noticed it was there.

Then, with no apparent pause or break in the gale of sand and dust that was around him, he suddenly broke free, falling out onto the ground. The opening to the grounds of his father's castle was in front of him. The wooden hole they had left through was now battered and torn. The other side was masked by a long wall of stone, which was further re-enforced by wooden panelling; as a child he had never properly noticed it. The structure managed at least to block out the ferocity of the storm behind it. He smiled to himself as he looked at it, sure now that he was safe.

After entering through the small wooden hole, Graciou found himself back inside the grounds of the castle. But now those grounds were different in so many ways, the heavy undergrowth masked his every viewpoint as he began to move towards the castle. Ripping the plants apart he made headway towards the back of the castle, where he hoped he might find an entrance. His fingers slowly began to tire as the grass was cut apart by them, his hands hurting more and more with each snap of the branches and curl of the leaves. But he persisted, for this was the one place where he might find the answers he was looking for, indeed most of him hoped he would.

The Storms of Acias

Ripping apart yet another clump ahead of him, he was presented with an opening into the castle, but it was an opening he didn't know and one that he had never used before. He stepped in cautiously, his view still masked all around by that of the overgrown plants and vines.

Continuing up the steps his eyes began to meet glass and broken pieces of wood littering the floor. Running up toward the entrance he remembered that this was the way that Barnabe had ordered Mary to take him. He retraced her steps back up the tower, which was what they had come down. As he looked down toward the staircase, straight into the face of a lidless set of eyes, a man's body sprawled out across the staircase, which had to belong to the person Barnabe had fought to quicken their escape. Its clothes were long since decomposed into that of the stone ground underneath and its flesh long since rotted away. The great picture of his great, great, great Grandfather long since dusted over and barely noticeable in the extremely dim light that bounced across the opening above him. Opposite him he could see the dining room, where all of this had started, its doors were wide open and he now noticed that the castle and indeed the rooms had gone into disrepair.

The walls were damp and there was a bad smell in the air. He moved along the coridoor, until he reached the staircase, which still seemed safe enough to walk on. Bodies littered its surface, but now that they were without their masks, they didn't seem quite so frightening. He walked into the dining room, quickly able to distinguish Harrass' body between the doors at the far end of the room. He stepped over to the body, searching it with his eyes for any clues that might reveal some sort of answer to him, but it only appeared that everywhere he looked he saw desertion and lifelessness. As his eyes descended to his chest he held back the tears that were becoming more and more present by the minute. In between the rib cage of his uncle's chest lay another cross, which looked much the same as the one he now held firmly against his chest.

Picking it up he jumped, as the head rolled over onto it's side, showing a large blow to the back of his head. How it could have been performed he was very unsure, but something of his death he was assured it must be. Then he thought to turn the cross over to compare that of Marcus' with that of his Uncle Harrass; each contained the same perfect shape, the same wood, the same glass and point on each of them, now both whirring round their points busily. But the writing was different from one to the next, Harrass's cross contained the words set into the wood yet again, each word repeated three times "Gracious, Excemaratis, Harrass".

    He knelt back against the cold wooden table leg, staring at both of the crosses and wondering what each had meant to their bearers, why would it be that his Uncle had carried a cross so much different to that of Marcus?

5

There were so many answers he still had yet to find, so many mounting questions that he knew not where to begin. Remembering his father's study and the great mahogany doors that barred their entrance, he got up and walked out of the dining room, to find them still intact and looking very much as if they had not been tampered with.

He broke its lock with a quick sharp knock into it from his shoulder, only to fall through the wood into a pile of rat infested nests, instantly picking each of them off and watching them run from the opening in the door that he had made. Shrugging the last of the sudden shock off, he walked toward the books and papers that still appeared to be intact, each bookshelf lined with many hundred year old books and artifacts, that had now long since perished in the cold.

His father's desk still appeared to be intact and removing a knife from the table he picked the lock of the drawer underneath which came off freely, as the rotted wood broke away under the blade.

Lifting the drawer out and placing it onto the table he found himself staring at only one letter, that had upon its front his name printed in dark silver bold capitals. Lifting it from its resting place and returning the knife to its opening, he sliced the letter open, unravelling the contents inside. Its scrawled and quickened handwriting read formally.

"To my son, Graciou.

I'm so sorry for all the secrets that have been kept from you, that you will by now undoubtedly know of. I hope that you find this letter when you are ready to find it and that you come to understand what it is I am about to say.

For the past twenty generations our family has lived and prospered under the shield of the great and formidable storm of Acias. I am sure that your eyes will have followed many of the paintings among the castle when you were a boy so many years ago, each one as I told you then, telling its own definitive struggle. I am sure that you will as the years have passed come to wonder of Harrass and his fate. Harrass was sent on a mission in the late evening to send a letter to one of the residents on the outskirts of the land. But it appears that he was ambushed and that when he got to the residents, everyone there was dead. As he ran back to the castle in his escape, he managed to guide the rest of the ambushing forces directly to where they wanted to be. But I cannot...I cannot let them get what they have come for...."

His writing began to change from its normal font face to that of a much more hurried tone.

"I must hurry now, for my life and yours is in perilous danger my dear son. I wish I could have told you more by now but the castle is filling with noise and commotion. Keep safe my son! Never let your heart wander!"

His writing trailed off scrawled and discontinued, the letter revealing only small vestiges of what he felt he should already have known. The Acias must have been the Storm that clouded the back of the castle but could strangely not be seen from the many balconies inside of it.

He placed the parchment onto the table and looked around the damp and gloomy room, the table appeared to have a stack of a hundred or so misaligned papers, and picking through them he found a partially written letter with the title:

"Mr and Mrs Grentshaw

I shall get straight to the point of this letter and make you aware of what it contains. This morning, just before midday, a sudden and disastrous storm devoured most of the village and the towns people that extend in and around it. We have taken measures to guard against such things happening again but we are incapable of making sure that another storm doesn't befall the people who live there. And if it does, the consequences may well be devastating to all. I must therefore, ask that the great shield of the Acias be called forth once more, for if the passage is blocked, then they shall not be able to attack. I know what I am asking is a very tall order but I..."

The Storms of Acias

The letter ended abruptly with its various letters and words appearing scribbled, compared to the other letter he had found. He knew not of a Mr or Mrs Grentshaw and knew not where they lived. Whatever the letter had been meant to safeguard against, it surely hadn't been able to. For all his years as a child he could barely remember playing with other children and he barely ever spoke to them, though he was always told to do so by the teachers he was with. He never felt any connection, as if something was truly masking that connection from him. Placing the letter abreast to his chest and leaving the other parchment face down where it sat, he got up from his chair, stepping over the rats that still littered the entrance, and placed a foot over into the hall.

He looked down the south corridor of the castle, which was blacked out and held no light at all. He passed by it as he walked to the central corridor before stopping. Ever since he had been small he'd been told not to wander into the southern corridor, it was so imprinted in his mind that each and every day he would walk past it and he would never wander near it. He felt the hair stand up on the back of his neck as he looked down it now. What was truly the reason why he had always been told to stay clear of it?

6

His eyes wandered over the floor as he progressed into the darkness that enveloped it. Stepping closer, he picked up one of the blacked out torches that stood on one of the walls next to him. The table next to it held lighting fluid and matches that he could remember his father using. As he began to light it, the torch burned black for a few seconds and then turned orange as it began to illuminate the floor at his feet, where each stone slab had been strangely uplifted at odd angles to each other. He walked across them trying carefully not to slip on the mossy overgrown slabs, each slab bringing him further from the stairs and deeper into the corridor, which was soon lit by a haze of light blue-stained glass. A gigantic window appeared to have been hidden behind the blackness and was illuminating much of the room.

As he looked closer he could see it was shaped in the form of a cross and across the centre of it…he stopped staring at the words and fumbled around for the cross that was around his neck. The words read "Graciou, Graciou, Graciou", he took out the cross from his chest freeing it from his neck and holding its blackened wood up to the blue haze, which bounced off the cross surface with great brilliance. The small pin that was set inside the glass top had stopped moving and was now set firmly upon the red line. He put it back down to his side staring up at the words as he read them. What did they mean?

Moving toward it his hands pressed outward, his fingers gently touching each word as if trying to feel something of what they meant. Suddenly, the words instantly changed from silver to red and began to flare menacingly at him. Running backward he smacked into something. He turned quickly to see what it was and as he did so was astonished at the result. In front of him stood the figure of a man he had seen before, the same man that stood in the staircase painting he had seen earlier. But this dark grey statue bore no resemblance to the vibrancy of colours that he had flagged his grandfather down with from his painting in the stairway. Indeed the statue looked to be an older impression of his grandfather. At the base of the statue there appeared to be a plaque.

The Storms of Acias

"This statue is in memory of our father Excemaratis the first.

He was the bearer of our faith and he made sure that through all our misfortunes, we upheld that same faith.

He was the giver of our fortune, no matter how far down we might have fallen; he would be there to bring us back up.

Above all else he kept the prophecy alive within each of us, our lives are indebted to him."

Below it was another inscription, more worn than the others and much less care had been taken over it, but none the less he was sure it had been put there for a reason.

"The prophecy has come true, Graciou is amongst us. Each of us now wait, we know not what we wait for, but wait we shall, through each conflict and each storm. Protecting the one thing we have upheld for so long, that of our son Graciou."

Now it was beginning to make sense, he knew not why he was the one being protected, but why he had been cloaked in such a shroud of secrecy for so long, matched their intentions. The first half described the obviousness of his grandfather's status within the entire community and that of his strength, which he had alone noticed from the picture. But the last part told of something he had never seen, did not know of and had never heard in discussion. Indeed he felt it somewhere close to the centre of his father's reason for protecting him all that time.

Without pause, he felt as if the corridor were moving, strange as he thought it was, he was sure of it, quietness quickly descended over him. The castle felt as if it was encroaching, as if the very building were waiting for something.

Then small dust trails began to form all around him, his eyes trailed the ceiling only to see parts of it were cascading down toward him. Flinging his weight forward, he tried desperately to clear the falling rubble, as he fell into the darkened corridor hitting the ground hard and heavy. Turning back he could see the room, filling with dust and smoke, debris blocking out all the light and forever sealing off his hope for any more answers. He pulled the cross out from his chest; it felt strangely warm against the palm of his hand. The red line was pointing in the direction of the stain glass cross; he noticed now, that it had actually moved from its first position to that of its new one, as if the very engraving had a mind of its own. His eyes shot back to the corridor, which was now completely dark and lifeless, his chest beginning to feel as if it was tightening, as if someone had got a clamp around it. He picked himself up from the dust-ridden floor and stumbled over the uprooted slabs that lay everywhere, in the broken and mangled corridor, continuing past his father's study and running out of the castle toward the gates.

7

From outside, no apparent disturbance or storm was guilty of the roof falling in on him. The pathway out from the castle gates was as he remembered it over fourteen years ago, littered with debris and pieces of stone, barely any signs of life around him. He could remember his father telling him to play dead at the foot of the gates and then hearing the strange noises all around him minutes later. Now he knew that all that time he was being protected, he wouldn't have been surprised if the distant shots that he heard were more dangerous than he first thought. His old school was dark and the hallway as grim as he could remember it, but each doorway was now shrouded in darkness and covered with cobwebs.

No building appeared to carry any life and nor did it appear anyone was left alive in the village. But that was something he had never quite understood, for the village on that day all those years ago had been completely free of people. From his home at the edge of the woods he had seen no disturbance like he had that day. It was as if his father's words on the parchment had been true, and that infact the attackers were searching for something, something they'd taken, or something they hadn't found. But either way they had not come looking for him at his new home by the woods, where it seemed to be so eerily cut off from the rest of the world. He looked down toward the south facing gates, which were flanked by two thick cream stonewalls. Each of the gate's doors were bent over and looked as if they were still about to fall so many years on.

Peering through, he saw only the overgrown roadway and some sort of carriage that was partially dismantled at the side of the road, but as he looked closer he could see that it was harbouring something behind it. Slipping through the gate's entrance he stepped through the two gigantic wooden doors. The path was moss-ridden and he could barely hear his footsteps as he trod ever closer to it, able to see several bullet entry shots that had been fired through the roof of the carriage.

His eyes darted across to the side where he could see a foot hanging limp and partially shrouded in cloth. Trying to stomach the unpleasant odour that had begun to seep up from the ground, he turned to find the body impaled against the back of the carriage; its face looked to be dry and the features of its skin appeared to have been sucked backward onto its skull. A gun lay limp in its right arm, the figure's eyes fixed upward at the sky. Then he remembered the cross that had been upon both Harrass and Marcus. Looking toward the man's chest he could see yet another cross and picking it from him he turned it over to find a most different engraving. The name read the same as the others, a set of three words, but his name in any form was not among them. It read, 'Grentshaw, Julian, Forester.'

Then he remembered it was upon a piece of his father's parchment that he had read it. Harrass had been sent to Mr and Mrs Grentshaw's property and was returning from there, having no idea what he had brought with him. Or had he… He looked up at the body and then around for any signs of life, as if trying to see if someone was watching him, but the place was dead, the overgrown branches and trees were the only faces that marred his sight. Taking the cross he placed it into a pocket on his clothes and moved off down the road leaving the carriage and that of his home village, which he hoped one day would not be quite so silent.

Turning the corner he found one of the larger manor houses, which appeared to have its own stables and armoury. It also appeared to be as dead as any other place he'd yet been past, but the outside of the house looked strangely kept, as if the vines and the overgrown moss had been held back, or even cut back. The door was slightly open and the garden looked as if delicate hands had pruned it. Stepping in through the doorway he looked around the gloomy dark hallway, his eyes darting to the large grandfather clock that was stood to his left.

A small tap to his right shoulder caused him to turn quickly, instantly unsheathing his blade.

"Don't be afraid dearey."

A pair of extremely dotty but fragile eyes stared at him through darkened spectacles. Her apron and dress appeared to match and were evenly laid out over each other, there also seemed to be the smell of some sort of food in the air.

"Who are you?"

Re-sheathing his blade he berated his nervous shock at her voice, wondering who it was she might be.

"It's not often I have guests, won't you come and sit in the kitchen?"

Moving into the room after her as she walked away, he entered into the kitchen, where a rack of freshly cooked cakes had just been prepared.

"Tuck in dear, they're not on display you know."

Sitting down and taking a cake, he returned to asking her who she was.

"Who are you madam?"

"I'm Mrs Grentshaw dear, but you can call me Rosie."

"Mrs Grentshaw? But you can't be."

"Why can't I be dear?"

"You live on the edge of the Acias."

Her eyes darkened over and she looked for a second as if she were going to faint.

"Are you ok?"

Her eyes darted back to his and she seemed to reorganise her thoughts, but he was sure the rest of the building had grown darker in shadow while his words had been spoken.

"Yes dear, I'm sorry, you said something about the Acias?"

"Yes the Acias, you live near it don't you?"

Her eyes, yet again, appeared to darken and he felt as if the room's shadows were beginning to darken over so greatly, that the light from the windows was in danger of being saturated by them.

"Don't you?"

"I used to, many years have passed now, it would be much better if I didn't speak of it."

"What happened Rosie?"

Her eyes bolted onto his, as if she were possessed.

"I remember the day your Uncle Harrass had appeared at the door and had given us the letter, my husband and he were sat down while I was looking out of the window at the Acias. They were talking about the letter and it faded into the background, as I was looking out into the Acias...the Storm can be so unpredictable... I saw a cloud forming which looked to be one of the phenomenon I've often seen from that window. But as I kept looking..."

Her face became strained, as if the sight of such an image in her mind was burning a hole through her brain.

"As I kept looking I saw a figure appear from the cloud, which started walking toward me. Its eyes were haunting, each one had a white centre, its skin was black and sunk deep against its body, and I wasn't able to stop...."

"Stop what?"

"I couldn't stop the creature from coming inside of me, it took over my body. From there on in, I can't remember anything, nothing but the haunting image of its eyes glaring down at me, its sharp white teeth bearing into my eyes."

Obviously, extremely distraught, she picked herself up from the table returning to the window, sticking her head as far toward the pane as she could. The room appeared to come back to its former life, each shadow receding and pools of light re-entering each corner.

"I forget how beautiful the sky is if I don't look at it, do you ever get that?"

"Sometimes, sometimes."

He didn't ask her to tell him anymore, but at least now he knew that a figure of some sort had entered her body. But if it had been there, then where was it now, then the chilling thought occurred to him. What if it never left?

"Rosie, before I leave I need to ask you one more thing."

"Yes?"

"Where did the figure go who entered you that day ten years ago?"

"He's gone now, he left me, he left…"

"Yes?"

"He left me at the front of this house, with the screams of my husband's lungs filling the air."

Emotionless tears began to trickle, each one cascading off her cheeks and falling onto her arms below.

"Oh God, I'm so sorry…I didn't."

"Do not be sorry, for I dare not be sorry with myself, for if I think I could have done something that day, I would never sleep."

As she stared out once more from the window, he looked around the room, catching sight of the open cupboard door that was beside him. Inside it, racks and racks of cakes had been stacked one on top of each other, each rack the same as the next.

He could see the fear in the house now, and the deranged way of her mind. He could see how she had become less of what she was and more of what she wasn't. Her eyes, now forever darkened by the images she had conjured with her mind, with the truth of a horror so present and true.

Standing up from the chair he looked over at her, unsure whether he should leave her or continue to stay in the house, but already she was lost, drying an already cleanly buffed plate from the side board. As he made his decision to leave, he doubted she would even know he was gone.

Opening the gate and shutting it gently behind him he looked back

The Storms of Acias

toward the house, where Rosie was nowhere to be seen, each of the darkened windows empty and lifeless. A cold shiver ran down his body as he looked up at the house, the previously pruned vines suddenly overgrown and heavy on the window frames.

8

His feet appeared to guide him down the road, each footstep bringing him closer to some new and unheard truth. He noticed that the small compass on the back of the crossthat had been guiding him, had begun to spin in all directions as soon as he left the house, neither the dial nor the red line meeting each other.

The trees that flanked the road had long since disappeared from it, leaving him completely unable to even see if the horizon was a mimic of the last mile or two of road that he had been walking along.

His mind was overrun by the talk he had had with the woman and he wondered what it was she had seen that day, and if indeed she had been taken over by it. If it had left her then where was it now? Where had it decided to lay its next trap? Why were there no traces of the force that had attacked the castle? Nothing made sense to him in its current state.

Then his eyes looked up from the roadway. Suddenly his ears filled with the tremendous rushing sound of some sort of impending wind and in front of him barely a mile or two away, a gigantic storm front was approaching, but as he waited and watched, the storm front didn't appear to be getting any closer, nor did it appear to be moving in any direction at all. As he moved closer it appeared to be covering something. Lead by its mystery he walked toward it, his gaze falling upon a small cottage-like house. Its doorway was unkempt and he wondered why Mr and Mrs Grentshaw had left the cottage in such a hurry. Checking both sides of it, he looked for a form of entrance to enter the house with, but all sides were covered by the ravaging storm in front of him. The thought also occurred to him; how could they have got away from the house if it was covered by the Storm? But then he remembered that this must have been the 'Acias' and if so its great movements he knew not of, nor who commanded them.

Only from his father's letter did he know anything of it. He checked back to the front of the house, still at the edge of the Acias; he looked for an entrance or a gap in the Acias. Whatever had caused both Rosie and Harrass to flee, he did not know. He picked up a small stone from the gravelled floor below, and threw it into the wind. As it was propelled farther and farther from his sight, it was carried off into the distance. The power was a sheer marvel to behold, and walking anywhere near it, would surely get him killed.

His hands gently touched on the worn face of the cross in his pocket, beginning to fondle it between his fingers. He thought what if,earlier, while standing in front of the stained glass cross, had it worked as a form of key? And if used again now, what effect it might have on the Acias? Picking it out from his pocket he ran his fingers over the words, "Gracious, Gracious, Gracious," holding it up to the Acias he waited for it to have an effect. But instead the cross lay cold in his hands, the Acias still raging behind it.

But had not both Mr and Mrs Grentshaw been the guardians of the Acias and its movements? Taking the other cross out of his other pocket which was clearly labelled, "Grentshaw, Julian, Forester," he put it up to the Acias. As ferocious and angry as it had been, it wilted from the sky, falling to rest around that of the house, littering the roof with sand and small rocks. The process was so quick and rapid that he stared at the cross in amazement, still having no idea at all how it could possibly do what it had just done. Now he had found the key, he wished he had not unlocked the Acias, for what had made both of them flee their home in terror, he dared not imagine. He stepped forward to it, the sun's rays beating hard and heavy against the porch. The handle was cold and worn against his hand and as he opened it, he was at first unaware of the scene that presented itself to him.

The room opened out in front, dim light cascading in through what remained of the broken shutters, a rolling light edging back and forth across the room, masking its true contents. He stepped inward, apprehensive of his every movement and he felt much alone, though he knew that the 'Acias' had been left to do its job. Whatever that had been.

Suddenly, light from the far shutter flew into the room, depicting the image of three dead bodies lying stiff against their chairs. Each looked as if they had starved, their faces black and their bodies dry, skin clinging against bone. Cringing, he pulled back away from them, the smell appeared to be subtle and there was only a faint trace of it in the air. From the looks of things, they had been tricked into staying inside the house and at an unsuspecting moment been entombed forever. But for a man and woman in their old age, it shouldn't have been quite so easy to pull off. He checked the room for anything of interest, to find a letter written in his father's writing. It was the letter he had started but not finished back at his house. The first half was much the same but had been slightly reworded, continuing from where it had stopped, it read…

"…I know that I am asking a very tall order of you both, but I am fearful for not just you and myself, but for everyone who lives in the shadow of the 'Acias'. These storms come and go, but with each new storm I feel as if they grow more precise and this one has come far too close to home. As always, I shall compensate in anyway I can. Harrass will partake as messenger and overseer of your actions, for reasons you know only too well."

The completed letter had shed light on the scope of the 'Acias' and its finer implications for the people it shielded. But it was obvious that the storm he had seen all those years ago was much more dangerous than he had then, and still to this day, understood. But the letter's completion, as well as the other pieces of information he had found and read, had not led to his father's whereabouts. The rest of the table was littered with what food they had been able to find, but it had obviously not lasted them.

Behind him the door was still open, the rest of the room appearing to be free of any other important items. He remembered the memory of Harrass and the state he was in when he last saw him. But there were no traces of blood on the stone floor and outside the 'Acias' was likely to have lifted any blood from the stone steps. He guessed that as he was fleeing from the building, he had been ambushed in his retreat.

Leaving through the open door behind him, the finished letter firmly set in his mind, he brushed past the opening to find the lock of the doorway had been broken clean out of its housing, and therefore the attackers must have lain into the Grentshaws as soon as the door had been opened. But their flight from the building was still a mystery. An enquiry with the old lady would prove quite fruitless, as he had noticed the way in which her eyes had wandered the walls while she spoke, mirrored by her thought process which was equally as erratic. Turning, he looked back at the house, sure it was now nothing of its former glory, the plants long since withered and died inside the picket fence that cut it off from what had once been the roadway.

Then just as quickly as the 'Acias' had disappeared, part of it started to wake once more. Startled, he fell backwards onto the ground staring at this new and more benevolent marvel; long columns and jets of sand-drenched air had begun to circle over the top of the cottage. Thundering down from the sky, as each jet began to pummel the house below, reducing its walls and ceiling, to less than rubble, collecting in a collapsed heap. It was as if the Acias had known, without any warning, that he had left the house. It was as if the Acias knew exactly what he had been doing. He stared at it, the last of the sand jets disappearing and falling dead, masking the house completely from anyone else's eyes; only one small piece of wood, protruding out of the top. If there indeed was anyone else out here, they would find nothing of interest now.

9

With the 'Acias' gone his view was marred no more. A long set of crag-gy rocks were strewn along the eastern edge of his view, with woods to the west and dunes stretching out in between the two. Then he recognised it as the spot where he had gone with Mary and Marcus that day, ten years ago. There was no storm, but he guessed the 'Acias' had been there in its presence. That must have meant the storm had at some point moved, from its place then, to its place now. But how had it moved all by itself, and for what reasons?

He had underestimated the storm's great intelligence and it must have been far more powerful than he understood.

He hoped Mrs Grentshaw's slightly erratic story was farther from the truth, for it sent a chill down his spine to think of such a figure, appearing from the 'Acias' the way she had described. Then the thought came to him; what if the figure she had described entering into her mind, had at some point later on entombed the men firmly inside the building? The 'Acias' commanded by herself? Whether it was true or not, he did not know. But if it was true and she had been taken over by this figure she described, though his mind was unable to believe it could be real, then she should still be under its control.

He thought he had not seen it when he first met her. But there was only one way to be sure. Even though he didn't like the idea, he had no choice. The house had seemed very unreal at the time and that felt strange to him. The road from the now ruined house was as it had been before; it was near-ly rubble now underneath his feet and the surface which was once there had long since eroded.

He could see his father's castle in the deeply set background, peaking out through the trees, where the rest of the town was covered behind. But what the Acias had been protecting all that time he was still unsure of. Nor was he sure what it had been protecting against. For over time everyone had seen a storm of some description appearing on the horizon, it was as if it had been finding ways around the Acias.

The Storms of Acias

The house wasn't much different than he had left it, but Mrs Grentshaw wasn't where she had been earlier in the day and with the sun setting the way it was, he felt it likely she had gone to rest for the night, but he still had to talk to her about where exactly the entity was. Even though she had told of its flight, he needed to know more of where it might have gone and the possession may have left an imprint on her memory.

The hallway was nearly pitch black as he reentered the house, the grandfather clock read eight thirty in the evening. Most of the walls were cast deep in shadow. The stairs were opposite to him and each rung swayed as if his feet were unsteady. The corridor behind him appeared to close and with the steady increase to his heartbeat he clutched the top of his blade firmly with one hand.

The top of the stairway had a small slither of light from the far end of the corridor, which laid a hazy line of orange light to the opposite end. It appeared that whatever family had once lived there were quite wealthy and a few of the pictures appeared to tell some thing of who they were. Members of his own family, mainly his father, were awarding them with various wealthy items such as the house itself and the stables, which had been built at a later date.

He continued down the corridor where he found one of the master bedroom doors, easily noticeable by its large golden handle and the fact that it had MB greyed into the wooden surface. Turning the softly golden buffed handle he found Mrs Grentshaw asleep on the bed inside and it appeared she had been for some time. Deciding not to wake her, he would wait downstairs in the kitchen till she awoke.

But just as he got the door half closed he heard a murmur from inside. Turning, he looked across the dark room to see what had made the noise, but nothing appeared to be there. Then again as he turned, he heard it once more, this time coming from Mrs Grentshaw's open mouth as she rolled onto her side facing him. The murmur had been incoherent and he was unsure what she had said, if she had said anything at all.

"Gracious...father...."

He'd heard the words, hitting him like an anvil at his heart, it's beat suddenly slowing down, as he felt the air around him begin to cool. It had been so long since he had thought of his father at any great length that he had put the question of hearing of him and his whereabouts nearly completely from his mind. Overtaken by this sense of longing for a father he had not now seen for over ten years, he shouted instinctively to ask about him.

"What of my father?"

She appeared to stir again, rolling onto her other side before answering. "Father...lost in storm...."

"Lost? Lost in what storm? The Acias is no more."

"So much...still untold."

Her words were coming through as pure and defined as any person he had ever spoken to. Whatever it was she was saying, it was coming from a side of her he had not seen or heard to date. Intrigued, he moved in closer.

"Where is my father?"

She waited this time, her longest yet, his ears resonating with the sound of his own voice in the air.

"Father...lost amongst the mountain plains..." a sudden rush of air filled the room, taking over her voice in an instant. "...Tired, so tired."

"Wait! How can I find my father?"

She strained greatly, searching for the words to his question, writhing on the bed as she did so.

"Use the cross of Graciou..."

Her voice was becoming heavily accentuated with the rush of air inside the room, beginning to sound as if her body was dying before him. She had spoken of a cross of Graciou, but he had never seen such a cross. Whether he had been meant for one or not, he was unsure, but wherever his name was used, it appeared to carry great importance with it. While his mind had been lost in the mystery of his birthright, her body had stopped moving. She had in fact become limp upon the bed, but as he looked closer he saw she had changed.

Her eyes had become white at the centre and her teeth bared for him to see. But her figure had begun to change as well, moulding to a new form, which mirrored the image that Mrs Grentshaw had already painted in his mind's eye. Its eyes were haunting; each one had a white centre, its skin black and sunk deep against its body.

With the image now set again in his mind, he walked over to the doorway slowly. But before he had managed to get over halfway, the figure had lifted itself from the bed and was facing him, darkness beginning to fill every corner of the room. Its eyes were just as she had described them, and he was unable to remove his gaze from them. Its teeth looked like pincers. But from somewhere inside him and he knew not where it came from, he found the strength and indeed the will to speak.

The Storms of Acias

"What did you do with Mrs Grentshaw?"

His hand subconsciously moved toward his blade once more. It stood unphased by his changing stance or verbal authority, which he was sure it would be able to feel.

"That is not of your concern Graciou."

Its voice was icy, like it was passing through the mouth of a small cave, barely audible in the howling wind at it's opening.

"You've made it my concern!"

"You are strong of will for one so young."

He didn't answer, waiting to see if he would falter, if the silenced reply would make him lose confidence, but he did not. Turning away from him he walked toward the edge of the bed frame, waiting till he was there to speak.

"I remember your father's face that day, as he left that study."

He felt his heart racing and suddenly as it had begun to race, he felt it blur away into nothingness. A sudden rage begged to build inside of him, one of deeply pitted anger.

"What did you do to him?!"

The figure turned back to him; face still as motionless as before.

"Nothing more than what I had to do."

His father's face suddenly shot into view, distorted and beaten before him, all sense of rationalisation quickly withdrew from every last vestige of his body. He drew his blade, swinging it high, to bring it down low.

Light was suddenly exhumed from the room and his blade tipped and fell as he became dizzy in the darkness, unable to balance neither his arms nor his legs. Following his immediate fall, a sharp crack filled the atmosphere in the room, as he heard the tinkling of his blade, each piece falling to the wooden floor. His eyes were marred by a bright white fog, which for all his might he could not see through.

Quickly, it began to fade from his vision, revealing a much more dusty room. Mrs Grentshaw's body was upon the bed, long since dead and decomposed, a note lying next to her. A sudden chill seemed to encompass him, as if he was going into after-shock. He placed himself on the bed, as it hit him, now unsure if his father really was alive, or if everyone was dead. Had he been talking to ghosts? What was happening to him? Then he remembered his father's words, which at the time had seemed so unimportant to him.

"Never let your heart wander!"

The words sunk into him and around him, soothing the sadness and loneliness he had not yet let himself feel. Once more he rested his head on the bed, now feeling abnormally exhausted and unable to keep his eyes open any longer. Without much effort his eyes fell firmly closed and he quickly fell asleep.

10

He woke to find that the sleep had refreshed his weary mind, which he had not noticed was becoming so drained. Next to him on the bed was the note he had seen earlier. He stretched his eyes, and then opening the note began to read it to himself.

"Before I am taken away from here, to somewhere of peace and harmony, it is my final wish that whom-so-ever reads this letter is to carry a message. For my dearest daughter Sophia, tell her that I and her father loved her until our dying breath and that I hope he managed to get you to safety."

He recognised now that was why the carriage had been turned over, for she had been inside it and he had protected her, but where she was now, he did not know.

"I know not of where the rest of our people have fled to, I believe somewhere to the north, but the grasp of what consumed me that day let me know no more. Its dreams have been too horrific for me to watch another instant of my life; it has finally ground me down to this point, farewell.

– Please take the item that I have placed in the drawer by my bed, for it will comfort Sophia, if she hears of this."

Beside the bed there was a small chest, with three drawers. Each drawer was worn and the paint had begun to peel from it, but in the bottom drawer lay a locket. Picking it up, he tucked both items into his clothes and gave the room one more brief look, before wasting no time in exiting the house.

As he came past the Grentshaw's carriage he found that the limp body of Mr Grentshaw was nowhere to be seen. He found it very strange, but he guessed that wild animals must have taken it in the night, as it had been there the day before. But it was strange, he remembered the body and why any animal would have gone anywhere near such a stench, he knew not.

Looking back toward the gate he could see the mountains in the background, a huge white tipped peak glistening in the sunlight, and somehow his heart leapt a little as he looked at it. No other place was fixed like it was, he knew not of anywhere else they would have fled to and seeing it as his only point of hope within this landscape, he headed toward it.

The gate was as he remembered it and he ran quickly over the broken doorway. The northern gatehouse was broken apart and the doors were knocked completely from their hinges. On the other side he could see carriages and carts knocked over. It appeared that someone had been attacked as they were leaving the town, but when or how many had left, he did not know.

Briskly he walked past, urged forward by the thought that his family might be close at hand, forever keeping the mountain as his reference.

Two days had passed and he'd as of yet found no one. The path he had been following had changed into a dirt track and long since faded, taken over by the long dark green grass.

Ahead of him a clearing was opening between two forests, as the plain ahead of him began to urge upward, toward the icy face above him. He stopped at the edge of one of the forests; ahead of him a small patch of grass had begun to move, shifting and swaying from left to right, but it was a faint swaying and he could barely notice it.

Stepping forward he crept over the spot, stooping over it, looking for some kind of animal, but instead he was met with nothing but grass. Kneeling, he shook the grass, his knuckle hitting something definite and metallic. Grasping whatever it was by the side, he recognised it as some form of helmet. Then the person who was its wearer stood in front of him. The man had a grey beard and by his arm a rifle, his entire uniform covered in patches of green grass, which had been his disguise. He stared at him, half astonished; he was looking back into the face of another human. Unable to hold back he started to speak.

"I've been walking for days. Are you really here?"

His voice was heavy and slightly frightened at his question being rejected.

"I'm real enough. But who might you be?"

The man's voice was fearful; he could hear it ringing behind his urgency. Beside him his gun was held tightly and his hand had not moved from the trigger. The gun was still pointed his way.

"My name is Graciou."

His voice was thin as if he had barely ever uttered his name before. The man's grip loosened on his weapon.

Noticing what was about to take place, Graciou quickly dived out of the way. Six more men from around him stood up obviously readying themselves for a fight. Gunfire blazed off into the distance, the man steadied his arm quickly and threw the weapon aside.

"Son! Are you all right?"

But as he looked up in the man's direction, at his startled and pale face, he saw he wasn't angry at him. He had dropped completely to his knees and was grasping him by both of his shoulders.

"Sir?" One of the others said.

The grey bearded man kept looking at him.

"You can't be Graciou, we thought, we thought you were dead," he replied, the man's face had regained some of its colour but he still looked pale.

"I am the son of Excemaratis the fifth."

The man's eyes narrowed slightly and he kept them fixed on him.

"I can see it now...my God, I can't believe you're alive."

He stopped, pausing at his own astonishment.

"Your father told us so many stories of you, what to look for, we searched the town when it was safe. He had given up hope. Mary did her job as he requested...and of Marcus?"

"He guided us as far as he could, but he died saving us."

It was a half falsity that he had uttered, but there was no need to complicate the situation with what had really happened.

"Tis a sad story indeed, he was one of the finest Captains I ever knew."

The man shook his head, his voice trailing off.

"I thought I wasn't going to find anyone."

He found himself once again in shock, unable to believe he had found someone.

"Well, you've found us now. We need to get you to the fortress, it's not safe out here."

He stepped up, still holding his shoulder with one hand, issuing the others various orders, as three flanked them on both sides.

"Is my father alive?"

His words fell heavy on the air and the Captain turned his head in mid-stride to answer.

"Indeed, yes, we'll get you back safe Graciou."

Then for the rest of their journey the conversation was silent. He surveyed each and every one of them as they concentrated without pausing for a single instant on their surroundings. The slightest movement was watched by one of the three soldiers. But as they moved closer toward where they were heading, his mind overflowed with so many questions. Unable to hold them back, he spoke.

"Where are we going?" Graciou said, having to shout over the wind that had begun to blow across them.

"To the mountain fortress, it is where the last of us remain. Ever since the attack we've been keeping ourselves safe up here. It's proved to be a worthy enough fortification, though we'd had our fair share of fighting. But enough talking for now, take these clothes so that you don't perish as we go higher."

One of the men handed him some clothes which he put around himself, though his feet ever increased in numbness as he continued to walk up the mountainside. The wind gradually changed into a blizzard as they went higher, blowing fiercely into the side of him. The rest of the men seemed quite comfortable, but were definitely clothed for such weather. Thirty minutes had passed, which he'd timed by the movement of the sun's fuzzy shape behind the thick snowy clouds.

"How much farther?" he asked, wondering where exactly they could be heading up here.

"Just over this dip and you'll soon be home and dry."

His eyes trailed over the dip as they walked in front of a completely featureless snowy face. Nothing moved and he was sure it had never moved in a hundred years. The grey bearded man was still at the front of them, watching as he walked forward, hand outstretched partially towards the mountain face, appearing to be clutching a cross that was held around his neck.

Without warning there was an immense bang from somewhere ahead, as a thin slither of golden light began to permeate outward from the opening that appeared. Each of the soldiers walked past him, but he remained fixed to the spot as he watched the doors opening. A quick glance around revealed something hidden in the blizzard, dark, but shaped much like one of the men he was with.

The Storms of Acias

"Graciou, come on boy, quickly."

The man was calling him from the edge of the doorway. Slowly he turned away from it, taking fleeting looks backward, before reaching the opening.

"After you, son…"

As he walked past the doors he felt his feet move onto dark brown marble underneath, gently merging into a fainter marble, which was coloured by the golden walls all around. The man was still behind him, looking out toward the snow drift, but he didn't appear to be glancing around, he appeared to be looking for something.

"Sir!"

The two large doors, which he now saw as separate sections of a material he had never seen before, were shutting closed, yet he was still stood outside the fastly closing door. But no less than a second later he was inside, as the doors began to bang shut, each layer locking from within.

"What was it?"

"Nothing, I just thought I saw something."

He looked over at him, smiling now, a lot more carefree than he had been before.

"This is the outside chamber."

Graciou looked around at the massive golden painted room, which seeemed to have its own unapparent light source. The room was so big he was sure that the castle would have fitted in it twice over.

One last bang from behind them issued, the last part of the doorway closing behind them.

"One more room through here and there will be a warm fire waiting for you."

His mind filled with the images of his childhood and the soothing warmth and safety he had felt inside the castle as a boy. He felt his mind being lulled into that same sense once more.

This time a much smaller but still quite impressive doorway opened on the other side of the room, inside was a chamber painted with silver.

"This is our secondary chamber. The entrance is just through here."

As they reached the other end of the chamber, the wall in front of them changed from light silver to a dark grey stone, which lifted upward for them to enter through. This was the last chamber; one more door was obvious at the far side of this, only a few yards from where he now stood. Once he was inside, he could see a fire raging and doorways leading off in separate directions from the main corridor. The grey bearded man turned to him and gave him a smile.

11

The grey bearded man turned to face the fireplace and he waited for whatever was going to happen next. Then he saw two men appear from a section of the wall, where he could have sworn there had not been a door before. The two men walked forward and stopped in front of the fireplace, their faces fixed heavily on Graciou...

"State your name."

The man's eyes didn't waiver or change from their present pursuit and he watched as the Captain gave his name.

"Kurubin Arnold"

He took out the cross that was around his neck, reading it's text to himself, "Gracious, Gracious, Gracious"

Both men embraced and then stepped back.

"Welcome back Captain! Where have you been? We expected you back three weeks ago."

So now he knew who he was, a Captain just the same as Marcus had once been.

"Well, it appears it was fate we did stay out."

The man looked confused.

"Oh?"

The Captain stood firm as each of them eyeballed him.

"Because stood next to me is the son of Excemaratis, Graciou."

Both men's faces went slightly limp and they looked flabbergasted, as they stared at him.

"It can't be!" one of them said in exclamation.

"Well it most definitely is, you'll need to call for his Father quickly."

"Of course."

Both men left, the Captain gave him another smile, which was different than the others, it was a smile of home, he was finally here. His ears met the sound of his father's heavy footfalls on the soft marble polished floors, as he came through the invisible doorway obviously unaware of what had taken place. His face was bearded and he looked older than he had looked when he was such a small child.

But he still wore the same clothes he had always done and as he rushed forward toward him, his arms outspread in disbelief, he could see the tears flooding from his eyes. Flinging his arms into his and holding the crushing embrace he stopped in the moment.

Finally, after all these long years re-united with his father once more. He pulled back his eyes level with his.

"I can't believe it's you."

He flung his arms around him again from where they had been on both of his shoulders and gave him another embrace.

"I thought you were dead," Graciou said, his father smiling at him.

"Are you all right?"

"Yes, I am now."

He smiled back, the two of them staring at each other for a moment, letting the moment sink in.

"I see Mary did as was told of her…"

"She did, we were safe for many years, but I was forced to leave her."

"It is sad to hear, but you're alive."

He stepped up with one arm still upon his shoulder and looked at the Captain.

"I will always be in your debt."

He began to kneel in front of him as the others began to follow.

"Please, do not kneel, from now on you shall each share a table with my family."

He turned back to the guard who had brought him in.

"Frelentine, we're going to have a feast, I want you to open the rations and tell the cooks to fill the kitchens. Tonight we will eat in the jubilation of my son's return."

His father turned back to the Captain.

"And you shall sit with us at the high table."

The guard known as Gregory turned away with his orders.

"Come son, we will get you a change of clothes and some food, you must be starving."

He led him toward the invisible doorway, which he saw now as a translucent dark brown marble exterior. As he walked through, it felt cold to his skin, but as he stepped into the room that opened out in front of him the chill was long lost in his mind.

"This is the main citadel, here we eat and here we stay safe from the outside."

The Storms of Acias

They walked down to the left, as the others turned down to the right of the white marble staircase that had opened in front of him. The banister rail was made of some form of buffed white stone. The ceiling composed of a gigantic chandelier that bathed the entire room in a white light. But the light was not harsh to his eyes, quite different it bathed his entire body with warmth.

They came to a small set of steps built into the side of the main staircase.

"This is our family chamber."

He traversed the stairway with his father behind him and opened the doorway, which opened out into a wooden walled study, its floor overlapped with different laced rugs, two leather wing backed chairs stood prominently flanking the sides of the roaring fireplace set between them.

"Sit down Graciou."

He did so and looked around the room like he was a boy once more.

"I'll get the tailor to come in later on and make you some new clothes. But first we'll wait on Barnabe. Are you thirsty?"

He nodded like he had done as a boy and then remembered that he was no longer that four-year-old child anymore.

"Yes, I've been walking for days, I could use a drink."

He barely knew how to speak to him it had been so long, but his father paid little attention to the fact and guided his every sentence with the same emotion that he had overflowed with, when he had seen him.

"So how did you manage to find the fortress? There were a few books lying around, but…"

He stopped him.

"No, I didn't read it from anything, after I'd left the manor house just outside the southern gate I walked back toward the town, I knew that you had left and gone northward, but I had no idea where."

His father nodded.

"So, you just happened to go the right way then, I guess?"

"Well I had a strange feeling that I might have been going in the right direction, but honestly, I wasn't too sure. I used the mountain as a fixed point, I didn't think I would find anyone."

His father smiled, glad still, that he was back.

"Well, thankfully Kurubin found you, he has a sharp eye, and no doubt he saw you coming along way off."

"Well, it was probably good I happened to come across Kurubin and his men, or they might not have found me at all."

His father nodded again in reply.

"So did you see anything? About the castle or within it?"

"I found your study, it was in a bad way, but I managed to read some of the stuff that was there."

"I take it you read my letter then?"

"Yes I did, but I couldn't figure out what it was that you were so keen to protect, you never made it plain that there was something in the castle that was so important."

Again his father smiled, but this time it was a wise smile, one where he knew more than Graciou did.

"Indeed, I was protecting you Graciou, I meant that letter as a safeguard against you coming after me. Until now it's been safe, it's been strangely quiet lately."

He felt as if his father were holding something back, as if something were missing.

"You sound worried?"

His father turned to face him, his eyes open wide, as if nothing was a-foot.

"No, its' nothing," quickly he continued. "Did anything else happen whilst you were there?"

"Yes…I found the Acias, it was covering the Grentshaw's cottage."

His father was quick to pick up on what he had said.

"The cottage itself was covered?"

"Well, it seemed to be protecting it, I'm guessing that's not where it was supposed to be?"

"Not generally, the Acias itself shields us from the various storms that come and go, though there had been more at that current time, none of us have any idea why."

He wondered why the Acias had moved, it was an easy enough explanation to say that it was protecting the cottage, but for what reason?

"Well I found several men inside, each of them had died from starvation, your letter was on the table, but it was really strange. It was as if they had been entombed there by someone."

"That is indeed strange. Was there anyone else there?"

"No, but when I went back to the manor house, I found Mrs Grentshaw inside, she was very talkative, but the house wasn't right, it felt cold."

His father's eyes narrowed slightly.

"How did it feel cold Graciou?"

"Like it was being consumed, the darkness in the house seemed limitless, like there wasn't any depth to it. At one point she even began to seem confused and resistant, I could have sworn the house got darker."

"Is that all? Was there anything else?"

"Well, this was before I went to the cottage, after I came back she wasn't downstairs. I found her in bed in the master bedroom, I was going to wait downstairs till she woke, but that's when she started to murmur, speaking about you."

His father put down the cup that was in his hand, leaning more toward him.

"She spoke about me, what did she say?"

"She said you were lost in the storm, but a lot of it was inconsistent, it didn't make any sense. I was going to leave again, but that's when I noticed her begin to change."

His father's eyes opened wide, as if he knew what was coming.

"Was it dark? White eyed? A haunting trance about it."

He couldn't believe he had just described the same figure.

"That's it!"

"What happened next? Did it try to attack you?"

"No, we spoke and it said a few things about you. But I didn't feel any fear with it, I kept on going, I stayed strong. Then it showed me your face, battered and bruised, that tipped me over the edge, I swung my blade at him. But the next thing I knew I was on the floor, there had been a blinding flash…"

His father stopped him, raising a hand quickly.

"There's something I need you to do Graciou, as quickly as you can."

He looked up at him, like he had done at the gates all those years ago.

"What's that?"

"I need you to close your eyes and search your mind, I need you to relax and tell me what you see. Tell me everything you see."

He nodded and closed his eyes, trying his best to relax now that he had stirred his mind so violently. But strangely he found himself lulled, probably from the lack of sleep into a dream state. Ahead of him there was a doorway, a buffed gold handle protruded in front. He had no idea where he was, but he was content none the less.

"What's there Graciou?"

"A doorway. I'm going to go through it."

He opened the door and found another dark room inside it, with a chair at the centre and a light above it, but the light wasn't covering any walls, for he could not see any.

"There's a light and a chair. I think I'll sit awhile."

And sitting he waited, for what felt like a good few minutes, before he could feel something quite different in the room with him. It was the figure and he knew it.

"There's something else in here…"

Then, startled, the figure jolted out into the light, it's sunken face grimaced and lunged toward his; he watched it, able to feel it's perspiration against himself. But it didn't appear to move.

"The figure's here." Graciou said with a tone of fear, his rage now diminished.

"You are very foolish for one so young, that blade could have hurt someone," it said with malice unlike anything he had heard before.

"What blade?"

He had no idea what it was talking about, but he knew exactly what it was.

"Do you think this is just a dream?"

As it moved slightly closer, he was able to feel the stench of it's breath upon him.

"I know I'm dreaming, what kind of a question is that?"

"Then why not look again."

And as he did so he found himself awake in the chair, with the sound of his father's voice breaking the silence.

"Graciou?! WAKE UP!"

"What's going on?"

"You were shaking like crazy, you've been out nearly three hours."

"Three…but it felt like…"

He could feel the sweat on his face and his father was stood in front of him, his back to the fireplace.

"Did you see anything?"

He stopped and looked at him, a strange fuzzy feeling circling around his head.

"Some man was there, it might have been the same man I saw, I'm not sure."

"What was it he said?"

"He was…"

The Storms of Acias

His father hadn't moved, but out of the corner of his eye something else quite different had moved. There, just in the corner of the room was the figure, the same one that had been in his dream.

"What is it?" his father answered back quickly.

"He's in the corner…"

In less than a few seconds he was scrambling off the back of his chair, trying to get to the other side of the room. Managing to see his father swiftly turn on his heel to face it, he propped himself up to get a better look at what had happened. His father was in the corner, with the figure cowering.

"Do you realise where you are?! DO YOU!"

His father's voice was tremendous and he even felt the air shake. It was as if he were verbally bashing it into submission and maybe he was. But all Graciou could do was sit slumped against the wall, trying to remove this now all too real thing from his mind.

12

The figure darted around his father, who had his cross held out, then he saw it look straight at his chest.

"QUICKLY! Graciou, GRAB THE CROSS!"

He felt a cold sweat pouring over his entire body as the figure began to fly toward him, the doorway to the right of him opened and several people rushed in, bullets beginning to hail in his direction.

"HOLD YOUR FIRE!"

His father's voice rumbled across the air, as several shots pinged off the wooden wall at the other end of the room. He grabbed the cross nearest to him and placed it against his chest. The written engraving on the cross started to burn him, causing him to shout out in agony.

"GOT IT!" Kurubin shouted and jumped into the air just as the figure was about to dive onto Graciou.

The figure fell onto it's side, as several other men walked in, his father grabbing the beast by the neck. The cross instantly released from his chest, but the pain was still excruciating, it was Marcus' cross that he had grabbed and his words that had burned him.

"GET HIM OUT OF HERE!" his father roared once more.

But it was not over, his father and the Captain were wrestling with the figure, as it grabbed Kurubin's arm, sinking it's teeth in. It's nails scraped against the wooden panels of the room and it's eyes hypnotised him; through the spectacle of his dreams and beyond, to his wildest most buoyant fantasies.

He woke inside a sealed white room, having no idea where he was. The pain of his chest still very present on his mind. A woman had been tending to him for the past few minutes, as he had felt her taking his pulse and bandaging him up. She walked past him giving him a broad smile.

"Glad to see you're awake Master Graciou. Will you be needing anything?"

"Not unless you think I need anything, but I'd like to see my father."

She nodded and left the room, he propped himself up on the bed and felt the bandage that was wrapped around his head. He guessed he must have banged it while he fell backward over the chair, and that was why he had felt so dazed. It hurt to think of what had happened but his father's face relieved that fact, as he walked in.

"How are you feeling?" his father said, looking worried for his well-being.

"Better than I did earlier."

"Glad to hear it."

He smiled and looked back toward the place where the nurse had been sat earlier.

"What the hell happened in there?"

"After you told me what happened, I knew exactly what it was that you had attacked, it was what we have come to call 'The figure'."

"Sounds like you've been calling it that for some time Father."

His face became saddened, half by the fact he had never known of the real truth behind all of this, and half because he had seen its horrors without knowing.

"Longer than you know…"

"So it possesses people and uses them as a kind of host?"

His father reclined back in the chair.

"That's right; very hard to notice, the reason we watch for so many of them, is because we don't know who might be carrying one. We have to be careful at all times."

Now he understood why Kurubin had to say so much when he entered the fortress, why there were so many locking mechanisms on the doors and so many different ways of fooling the enemy.

"Has it ever happened before?"

"Yes, many times, the figures are extremely manipulative. They toy with the person's mind and bend reality so far and so great, that the person is unable to detect whether they are real or not. But once you pointed out what was in the room and were so driven by your fear, you bounded off the chair. If you hadn't have done that then it could have been much worse for us all."

"How exactly did I help?"

"The figure relies on the person not knowing they are there, without that they just flee, perish or pass on to another. In this case you were somehow nullified by its presence, and seeing as you attacked it before, your aggression showed that you could see it. You weren't ready to accept it's capabilities and it's fear."

"They sound pretty dangerous, I hope I don't ever meet another. How did Kurubin get hurt?"

His father turned to look at another bed that was lying past him on the other side of the room.

"The figure bit him, he was particularly vicious, practically rabid, it wouldn't surprise me if he hadn't met another of his kind for all the time we've been apart."

"Hang on, if Kurubin's here and you're not detaining that thing, then where is it?"

He smiled.

"As soon as you left that room it perished and withered in our very hands."

"But you said it can pass on to another as well?"

He straightened his face somewhat.

"My anger was not enough to scare you both into seeing it? Besides, the others were all soldiers, they had seen the figure's work before."

He gave a short laugh and Graciou followed.

"True enough, I'd never seen you like that, ever."

"Just another thing I had to hide from you as a child, I didn't want you aware of any of it, not until you were ready. I won't hesitate to make sure you know everything about it from now on."

"Well, I'm glad it's gone, I was terrified once I found it in the room, but I hadn't been before."

"It must have said something to you while you were dreaming, you were hazy at the end."

What it had said was merely an enticement to anger him, nothing more.

"Anyway, get some rest and I've delayed that feast for a few days 'till you're well enough to eat with us."

His father got up from the chair.

"No, wait, I'm well enough."

His father laughed as he replied, "Look, however courageous you might be, the Captain still needs his sleep. Oh, and before I leave, I want you to know I've never seen someone act as quickly as you did in that room today, I'm proud of you for that."

He exited the room without a second glance back. Letting his head dip into the soft white cushion he rested his mind, letting the thoughts of the past week spill out into his conscious mind, along with the questions of the

The Storms of Acias

past ten years. As he slept the recollections of his past. Grew with intensi-
ty, as he fell farther and farther into the drifts of sleep.

13

He woke, the room was dark and whatever light had been emanating from the walls had faded. The Captain was across from him, dimly set in the near-pitch blackness that surrounded him.

Getting up he put on the clothes that had been laid out, they were new and slipped on much more gracefully than the others had. The fit was quite elegant, resembling his old clothes in nearly every manner, apart from the fact there were fewer pockets. His head felt better already and he was sure it wouldn't be long before he was back up on his feet properly.

But his chest still hurt as much as it had yesterday and he was careful not to touch the bandage as he put his clothes on. The doorway was barely a few metres from him; the nurse, the same as before, did not appear to be in the room. Wondering what might be happening, Graciou sneaked out, being careful not to wake the Captain.

There was no-one outside of his room and nobody on the staircase. But as he looked across, he could see his father's quarters were open and light was jutting out from them. The citadel light was now much dimmer; he guessed it must have been evening, for the light much resembled that of moonlight. As he got closer to his father's quarters he could hear talking from inside. How he could hear he was unsure, but someone must have been shouting, or he would not have heard it from this distance. Looking back around the citadel he could see nothing but himself. Whatever they were talking about, he wanted to know.

They were indeed shouting as he got closer. As it grew ever louder and he started to pick up vague parts of the conversation, the voices sounded familiar and one of them he identified as his father's. They all sounded extremely annoyed about something, he drew in closer and waited in a concealed shadow by the door, listening to the conversation.

"I can't believe this has happened, did you see him when he came in here?"

"Yes I saw him, he looked fine, and for God sake was I supposed to have got rid of him?"

There was a pause.

"No, no, of course not. I just can't believe they got inside."

"Well they did get inside, whatever the consequences, we're going to have to deal with that fact."

Another voice interjected, it was calmer and sounded female, in fact it sounded a lot like the nurse.

"Graciou's asleep now, but when he wakes, I think it's time you let him know about all this Excem. We don't want him to hear about it suddenly, he's not that little boy I knew anymore."

There was a pause and then his father spoke.

"I know that, but you know as well as I do how terrifying these things are, you know as well as I do what they're capable of, you know the carnage and bloodshed we have had to endure for centuries. He might have seen it, he may even understand it, but if there are still pieces of information I need to conceal, I will," he sighed. "I must protect him."

Without warning he began to hear footsteps coming from the door, he ducked back into the dim shadow by the wall. Watching the shadow of the nurse walk out of the room, he could tell she was annoyed, by her stance. She quickly sped across the citadel toward the room he had been in, any minute now she would know he was out. He quickly concentrated on listening into the room, to see what else it was he could overhear.

"You know she's right Excem, you might be my big brother and we've always had Graciou's interests at the forefront of everything we've done. But maybe it's time to let go of myths and fantasies, time…" he was stopped and he knew now that it was the voice of Barnabe, he sounded old and somewhat changed.

"Are you insane? Let go…refute…destroy the faith we've laid in the prophecy for over five generations! Just because you want to give up now?"

His father's voice had risen above that of Barnabe's.

"Well I won't do it Barnabe, Graciou's the last piece of this myth you speak of, I know that everything we and my father, and his father before him have believed in. I know that it's all been worth it. All we have to do now is look after Graciou, that's all, but we still need to keep his interests uppermost."

Barnabe sighed and his voice appeared to become muffled.

"But none of us know what we're waiting for anymore, people are in low spirits, our military consists of nearly twenty men. I'll stick with you on this, because I've never done any less than that. But think about what you're doing to Graciou, or what might be Graciou's right in all this."

"Do you know what he said when he came in here?"

His father was defiant, but he could feel the overwhelming drive within him not to let go of what he was speaking of, whatever it was in it's finer glory.

"No, what?"

"He said he confronted that figure, he confronted it and drew his blade to it, that ghost knew something and I have no idea how...."

His voice was cut short, by another much closer to him.

"And what would you be doing Master Graciou?"

Next to him stood the woman, she was wearing white and looked a little annoyed by the fact he wasn't in bed. In the room, he could hear footsteps walking his way.

"What is it?" he heard his father say.

"Graciou, he's outside."

His father walked out, with Barnabe looking older than he sounded.

"I feel a lot better, I was trying to..."

"Don't even try lying, I'm guessing you heard all of that?" his father bolted back at him.

"Well maybe if you weren't making so much noise, I wouldn't have come over."

His father looked slightly taken aback, but maybe now his father was starting to see the difference in him, the difference that time had placed there.

"You weren't supposed to hear any of that Graciou..."

He stopped and looked at Barnabe.

"Maybe it's time now Excem, time we told him?"

His father picked him up by the arm.

"If you think he's well enough?"

She looked at him as if he had asked a stupid question.

"Well he looks fine currently, I'll be in the med ward if you need me."

She walked off looking disgruntled, still reeling he guessed from his father's persistence.

Each of them sat down in the room and he aired his most pressing questions.

"I want a straight answer to this, why am I so important?"

His father spoke, with Barnabe watching from the chair next to him, There was a pause, but he knew his father was going to tell him, he had no choice.

"When your mother and I had you, we had already been given a name that under certain circumstances, we were to choose," he stopped, Barnabe took up the lead.

"But the reason they got given the name in the first place, is because they were told to. A long time ago, someone came to your fifth great grandfather, he told him about you and he said that you would need to be named Graciou."

He knew about his grandfather, for now the engraving on the plaque made more sense than it had before.

"Yes, that's right, I read the plaque where his statue was. I didn't really understand it, but now it makes sense."

"That plaque has been there for many hundreds of years, it was presented as a token of goodwill to our family tree by the people of the town."

His father had taken the lead and paused.

"Did you see the part underneath?"

"Yes, it told of me..."

Suddenly, he remembered it and things were beginning to make sense.

"Like you said, it's about you. You're the Graciou prophesied. It sounds dramatic, but really none of us know what it means. You're at the centre of this prophecy and have been for five generations."

Slightly shocked, he wondered for a moment how he could be so cared for, but then again, he always had been.

"I can see how I fit in, but I don't feel as if I'm that person..."

Barnabe looked over at his father for a fleeting second, before returning to the conversation.

"Well...I guess you won't yet," his father interjected.

"Whenever you feel you understand it Graciou, we'll be ready to listen. But this is the reason I never wanted to tell you about any of this, because I was sure you weren't ready for it."

His father seemed to remember something suddenly.

"The other day Graciou, you had that cross in your hand, where did you find it?"

For a moment his chest ached at the burn and he gently touched it.

"It was Marcus' cross."

"Did he give it to you?" Barnabe interjected again.

"Well, no. There was a reason that I had to leave Mary, it was because Marcus had come to the house, but he wasn't Marcus anymore."

His father looked slightly astonished.

"Marcus came to you? There?"

"I didn't believe it either at first, but after I saw him, he wasn't the person I thought he was. But it was Marcus all the same."

"Why wasn't it him Graciou?"

"His body was contorted, like it had been tortured or mutilated in some way, it was horrible to look at. That was when he asked me to kill him."

"And you did?"

Both men were listening intently; Barnabe seemed to know what was coming.

"I couldn't do anything else, he said time was running out, he made out as if I was in danger."

"You couldn't have done anything less son."

Barnabe lifted a hand to his shoulder.

"Indeed you could not, it seems Marcus was long gone. But you say he had a cross on him?"

"Well, once I looked at the body I found something around his neck, which I later saw as the cross. It's the same one that I used yesterday."

Barnabe removed a cross from his neck, which he presented to Graciou.

"Is this what it looked like?"

Graciou looked at it for a second, reading the words "Gracious, Maria, Gracious".

"Nearly, the second word is different."

Barnabe looked to have completed what he had set out to achieve.

"It's Marcus' cross all right. Maria was your mother's name Graciou."

Graciou looked up, it was the first time his mother had been mentioned.

"My mother? My mother's name was Maria?"

"Yes, it was," his father said, still looking at the mirror that adorned the mantelpiece, an obvious sadness in his voice.

"What happened to her, father?"

Graciou could remember, but in all the time that had passed since the event, it had become blurred and faded in his mind. Barnabe seemed to take over nearly instantly, but his father stopped him.

"No, wait Barnabe, I want to tell him this myself."

Barnabe gave a held back sort of smile, returning to his chair while he spoke.

"When you were very young...she..."

The Storms of Acias

His father's eyes had already begun to fill with tears and he could see how much it hurt him to think of it.

"She was killed at the hands of the storm, you had only just been born a few days earlier."

He had both of his hands clasped together and was looking down towards them, as if his words had barely given any credit to her death. Though he was sure he had wanted them to, in every possible way. Graciou got up from his chair, going over to his father and comforting him as best he could. Barnabe gave him a firm smile, which he could see was holding back a flood of tears.

14

The sun woke him the next day and the memories of the previous day came flooding back. His father was asleep in the chair and it appeared he had been moved onto one of the beds. Barnabe was sat beside him in the chair, looking as if they had not moved all night, the small table in between the two chairs laden with a bottle, only one quarter of its contents left. For the first time he'd seen two sides of his father, one side was a man of great authority and a man who understood his foe greatly.

The other was of a man who could not easily talk of his deep emotions, but upon his return those emotions had come to the forefront of his mind and he was unable to stop them. The both of them had told him nearly everything they knew and though he still had questions, the larger pieces of the puzzle had been set. He guessed that his name had appeared the same as it had on the cross in the stained glass room, though why his memory had chosen only now to see that particular image, was very strange.

His mind was brought back to the present, eyes flicking across the room. The door appeared to open down away from him and someone had stepped into the main room.

"Hello"

She turned the corner and looked in his direction, she was a slender girl, of about his age, and her hair was long and dark. It met her hips.

"Hi," she said.

"Did you need my father?" he replied bluntly, still trying to focus properly.

"No. Barnabe. But I was told to come here this morning." He smiled at her.

"I think they're both asleep currently, what was it Barnabe wanted?"

She carried on speaking, with the same carefree tone she had before, which he found pleasantly reviving to the memories of the previous evening.

"Well, I got a message from Barnabe, but he didn't say why, just said to call in here."

He nodded, unsure quite what he should say next.

The Storms of Acias

"I can always wake him for you?"

"No I may as well come back later when they're awake."

Then he thought, there wasn't really much point staying here alone till they woke.

"Hang on…"

She turned back.

"Yes?"

"I don't suppose I could come along could I? I don't think either of them are going to be awake for quite awhile."

"Sure, I'll wait outside."

She smiled and left the way she had come in.

A few minutes later he was ready, closing the door behind him. Her back was turned and she was overlooking the railings.

"My name's Graciou." He said it without remembering that for the past ten years he hadn't even been around.

Startled by the name, she turned around.

"Graciou? But you're supposed to be…" she stopped, knowing what it was she had been about to say.

"I came in yesterday with one of the parties."

She looked now as if she knew what he was saying.

"Hunting parties?"

He knew that it hadn't been, but no other party could have left the complex and seeing this, he knew she had not been told the truth of it.

"Yes, that's the one."

He raised his eyebrows to enquire about her name and she replied with the answer.

"Oh, my name's Sophia, sorry."

She stood there for a moment, waiting for him to say something, but he was still sifting through the thoughts in his head, who had he known by that name?

"You must be thinking you're talking to a ghost now…" Graciou said. She smiled.

"Well not really, you're real enough, it's just that after your father looked for you, most of us thought that was it. We've been living here for quite a few years now, we've had to ration for the past 5 years, we've not been able to eat as freely as we'd like. Though I hear we might be having a feast soon."

"If my father says it's going ahead, we should be, yes."

She stopped for a second, looking out over the citadel and changing the conversation.

"I guess you're wondering what this place is," she smiled, he only knew in part, but didn't have to answer. "What would you like to see?"

"Well I only know the way in..." he smiled and she laughed a little.

"I'll show you the rest then."

They walked off around most of the citadel and she showed him the houses that were set into the sides of the large stairways, each able to hold at least five people. Each house was like his father's, but bigger. She showed him the different areas where food was stored and prepared in huge stone towers, and the servant quarters along with the chefs and finally the lower floor where the main eating area was.

They had both stopped at this point and she had only spoken about the areas while they had been walking, not bothering with small talk.

"How often do you all eat here?" he said, trying to spark up another line of conversation.

"Every few weeks, it's usually with the entire citadel. We only fill those three tables over there though."

He looked at the tables, each must have carried fifty or so people, but the amount that had once lived inside the town's walls was much higher. There were roughly nine large tables set out across the marble floor, but he was still unable to comprehend that quite so many had died in the years that had passed.

It was a question for his father, for when he had been walking through the town, he had never felt that the destruction had killed anyone. Merely made a nuisance and that was all.

"Just three tables?"

She looked at him, as if it had always been that way.

"Yes, just the three."

He still couldn't place her name among the others, but he kept trying to remember who it was.

"Who are your parents?"

She had turned to face him, they had just been leaving the main dining area, which was a sunken basin that jutted up and out onto a circular path-way.

"I...I was split up from them as a child."

She looked very upset that he had even mentioned the fact.

"I thought...sorry to hear that."

He hadn't meant to upset her, but it was obvious that she didn't cope well with talking about it.

"I try not to think about it too much, my memories aren't as fresh as they used to be."

He knew only too well what it had been like, even if he had repressed most of those feelings 'till yesterday.

"I can empathise with that."

She seemed to perk up, even though she still didn't know at what level he was empathising.

"I guess that's true, where have you been all this time?"

Sophia didn't appear to know that much about it, but she knew he had been missing.

"Well, I got split up from my father, you probably already know that It's been thirteen years since I've seen him, for the past week I've been wandering outside not even knowing if I was ever going to find anyone again. That's when Kurubin found me."

"It seems we have something in common there at least, you've been gone for a long time Graciou."

She had spoken as if she had been trying to find him for years and yet he could not remember seeing her before.

"Let's go back up to your house, your father and Barnabe should be awake by now."

"You're probably right."

Letting her lead, he followed.

They walked up past the different sections, talking intermittently about them and what they were for. But nothing more of either of their lives passed between them. Slowly his father's quarters drew closer and no less than a few minutes later they were stood outside. They had both stopped and he had turned to her.

"Your name seems so familiar, I can't think who it is though, must sound stupid to be saying it. But I can't place it."

She shrugged and turned to open the doorway, he had expected some sort of answer, but it appeared she didn't think he needed one. Inside, his father's seat was empty and he could hear talking from the other room.

"Where is he then?!"

His father was shouting, the same as he had been before. He was sure if he had seen Sophia he would not have been shouting.

"Look calm down Excem, I'm sure he's close by," he heard Barnabe mention inside.

Graciou called out, to stifle his shouting. "Father…"

He walked into the room, his father's height looming over them. But as soon as he saw Sophia, his eyes changed completely. He came over to her and kissed her once on the head.

"How are you Sophia?"

"Well, thank you," she smiled at him. He could see it was a smile much more like he would have given to his own father.

He guessed that since she had been separated from her parents, his father had looked after her.

"Barnabe told me to come here this morning. But you were still asleep."

He looked down at Graciou for a second, as if he had done something wrong by not telling him where they had been, but she appeared to cover his back.

"I was showing Graciou the Citadel, seeing as he's been away for so long."

Barnabe's voice entered the room now he was awake.

"Good morning Sophia."

He paused for a second looking at them both with a vague trace of a smile and continued.

"Yes, I did send for you that's correct. Seeing as both of you are of the same age and it's about time Graciou and yourself got your own crosses. I thought it would be best if you teamed up together."

He hadn't been prepared for this, what was the cross all about? Intrigued, he listened further.

"I would say yes Barnabe, but…" she looked at Graciou.

"Well I guess maybe if you think it's right."

Why she was less than happy about it he had no idea.

"You're the only two in the citadel who were born in the same month as each other, it only seems right that the both of you should work together on this. You can help each other out with the various trials."

That was an interesting statement, for if they had been born in the same month, then he would have met her at some point. He remembered that each child in their first year would meet the other children of the town, that way each generation got to know each other and could help each other out, plus the fact that it made a much tighter social group. But he could never remember meeting her.

"Alright, if you think we should."

He was happy she had agreed to it, for the fact she'd gone through some of what he'd been through would in time mean they might be able to talk about it.

"Your first trial should be to learn more about the storms of Acias and the Grentshaw's."

Suddenly he remembered who it was, it was Mrs Grentshaw's note that had talked about Sophia, it was her daughter!

"That's it! I know where I've heard your name before."

Sophia looked startled at his out-burst and he calmed himself as he carried on, but before he could, Sophia interjected.

"I think that's a WONDERFUL idea Barnabe."

She appeared to beam at him, as he wondered exactly what it was she didn't want him to say.

"Why don't you show Graciou the library Sophia?" Barnabe said with ease, not paying too much attention to the fact that Graciou had made the outburst.

"Graciou?"

He paused for a split second, but didn't want it to be noticed and rushed his reply.

"Sounds fine to me, I can't remember what I was going to say anyway."

It was a lie of course, he hadn't forgotten at all.

Outside he stopped her.

"I do remember where I've seen your name before Sophia."

She pulled in closer to him.

"You do?"

"Yes, I couldn't say it in front of my father, he wouldn't have let me." he continued, "I know your name because I found your mother."

She pulled away.

"What do you mean you found her?"

"She'd left a note where I found her, it said that if I were ever to find you, that I was to let you know that they always loved you, she also gave me this."

She pulled further away.

"What? No…I can't.."

Tears had started to run from her eyes.

"I'm sorry you had to hear it like that…"

She was obviously deeply distressed by what he had said. She started running just as he had begun to stop speaking.

"Sophia wait!"

But it was too late, she was already out of sight. He knew how she must have felt about it, suddenly being told her father and mother loved her, it had been such a long time since she would have spoken with them. Remembering the locket he had been told to take with him he checked his pockets, but his clothes had already been taken off him in the nursing bay. Quickly, he walked over to the nursing room, where he found one of the nurses sat down just behind the door.

"Anything wrong Graciou?"

She smiled at him as he entered, looking ready for a wound or some sort of pain.

"No, I'm fine, but do you know where my old clothes are?"

"Of course, they're just here in this box."

She placed the box on the desk. He began to sift through the clothes that were in it, finding his old jacket, where he had placed the locket and the letter.

"What is it you're looking for dear?"

"Something I needed to give to someone."

He wasn't about to tell her quite what, just in case she wanted to take it back.

"Found it…"

His hands had met the golden buffed locket, which felt smooth under his hands.

"Thank you," he said, smiling as he quickly left the room.

"Goodbye…"

Her voice was quick to trail away, as he walked down toward where Sophia had entered her quarters. It was fairly dull inside and he could tell that the luxurious nature of his father's quarters could not be permeated throughout the rest of the houses. Inside the house there lay a bed in the corner, where he found her, half curled upon it and turned over toward the wall. He could still see the tears on her face from before.

"Sophia, are you all right?"

She turned over and wiped her eyes clean of the tears, then stood up slowly in front of him.

"Yes... It was just a shock," she continued, beginning to wash her face, in the washbasin as she did so.

"After we got separated for good at the town, I never thought I'd see anything of them."

He smiled kindly, in acknowledgement of her sadness, looking for the locket in his pockets.

"She also told me to give you this, so that you could remember her."

She presented a hand in front of him, which he placed the locket into. Her eyes instantly fell on it, as if absorbing the memories that it held.

"She would often give this to me when I was young, she said it was one of the oldest things she'd kept. Thank you for bringing it to me Graciou."

"No need to thank me..." he said, with ease and care in his voice.

She looked up at him: Her eyes were dark brown, accentuated with hazel. They stared at each other for a second and then she walked past him to the door.

"Well, we better get on with what Barnabe told us to do."

He walked over to the door as well, smiling at her inability to open up to him, but the fact she had come close was enough to make him feel as if she were not quite so sad about hearing of her parents.

"Yeah, I guess we'd better, I can tell you about the Storm though, seeing as I've seen it myself."

"You have?"

He then proceeded to tell her all about it, leaving out the parts about the dead bodies, but being as truthful as possible. He wasn't about to knock her emotions into yet another spiral. They entered the library, where they found a few children being looked after in the far corner of the room, a few older men and women were dotted around reading various things. But mostly they seemed quite withdrawn and happy to read in solitude. They walked around the old library and up and down the various dusty and dirty racks, until finally they found some books on what they were told to research. There was only one book on the 'Acias' itself, but he guessed it would be more than they needed, not to mention that he had seen most of it himself.

They continued to both read the book as the hours went past, not really talking too much about the content. It stated that the Grentshaws were its Guardians and used the cross of 'Grentshaw, Julian, Forester' and 'Grentshaw, Rosie, Forester' to command the storm. Much of what had been added to the end of the book was about the family's death and the

Acias' last fight against the great dark.

Whilst reading it he felt that he should re-write the last few pages, so that they gave a more accurate picture of what truly had happened, for he had been there himself. No sooner had he put it back than at least two adults had come along, both opening the last five pages, reading eagerly as they did so.

Once they had got back to her quarters and it felt like hours had passed, he felt himself feeling glad of the time they had spent with each other. He was standing at the bottom of the steps and she was at the door.

"I guess I'll see you again tomorrow," she said from the top of the steps, looking apprehensive about the answer.

"Sure, I'll find out what Barnabe wants us to do next. I'll call on you tomorrow."

She nodded, giving him a nervous smile and closed the doorway. He walked back up to his father's quarters and opened the door: Both Barnabe and his father were deep in discussion when he entered. Barnabe turned to look at him.

"Graciou, how did it go?"

"Very well. We found out a lot about the storm and I added something to the book about Mr and Mrs Grentshaw. Seeing as no-one seems to have any idea what happened to them."

"Good, well I won't quiz you, I'm sure you've told her about the Storm and that you both know how it works."

Barnabe turned back to his father, but he was waiting for the next trial. Standing, he waited for him to turn back with some sort of answer.

"Ahh, you want the next trial I guess."

He smiled in acknowledgement.

"I think it would be best if you both looked at the way in which the cross has some very interesting properties."

He looked at his chest, which had not hurt once for the entire day.

"I bet that burn still hurts?"

He looked surprised.

"No, actually it's stopped, I mean there's no chafing. I can't even feel it."

"That's a very quick recovery, last I heard that burn was deep."

"I know, it's strange indeed, but it doesn't hurt anymore for sure."

"All right, well if it starts to hurt it's probably best to ask the nurse."

15

Walking into the other room, he removed his cloth shirt, taking care not to brush against the bandage across his chest. The burn which should have been there, the same as it had before, had now completely disappeared. He could not understand it, how could it heal so quickly? Putting his shirt back on, he walked out of the house to find the nurse. The med ward was fairly empty. The Captain was just getting up from his bed as he walked in, being helped by the woman he had seen earlier.

"Hello, Graciou," she said, without a second thought.

"I had to leave quickly earlier, sorry about that."

She turned as he finished, smiling.

"No need to worry, I don't offend that easily."

"Was there anything?"

He turned away from the Captain as he said it, but he doubted very much he would hear.

"Well yes, you know that burn from yesterday?"

She looked up, his tone of voice troubled, as if something were wrong.

"Yes, what's wrong?"

"Well I just looked at it earlier...but it's gone."

Unable to believe it for herself, she moved to his shirt, which she began to tug off, he held it up so she could see his chest.

"How did this heal so fast?"

Unable to answer, he rebounded the question back at her.

"I was going to ask you that question."

"This is very strange...miraculous...I don't see how it could have healed so quickly."

Behind them the Captain was roused and walked over, he looked better now, but he could see that the figure had indeed made some sort of mark. He gave Graciou a smile and took a look for himself.

"Is that the same burn you received when the figure was in the room?"

"Yes, well it was, I don't know what happened, but since last night it's healed itself," he continued, turning back to the nurse.

"I was going to ask you if you put something on it."

"Well, even if I had put something on it, a burn takes along time to heal, I was expecting it to scar quite badly."

He put his shirt back on. Still confused by what had happened.

"I guess it's a blessing for now," the Captain had said.

"If I can excuse myself," Kurubin said.

She looked at him, as if he had no right to assess his own health, but she wasn't going to boss him around.

"Of course, please do."

Kurubin passed him by the door and was already outside of his sight, by the time he came to speak once more.

"So you've got no idea why this might have happened?"

"No, but like the Captain said, I'm sure it's not a bad thing."

She gave him a comforting smile and he turned and left the way he had come, saying goodbye to her as he left.

Outside, he found the Captain with his hand on the railing.

"How's the arm Captain?"

"Please call me Kurubin, Graciou. No need to be too formal with me. The arm's a lot better, it will heal quite quickly I should guess."

"You make it sound as if you've been bitten a lot."

He turned around to him, his face looking a lot more serious.

"That figure in there is more deadly than either of us could ever be Graciou, even more deadly than your father's own blade. I've seen a lot of fighting in my time, and to answer your question, I have come out, as have many, battered and bruised from the event."

He smiled, as if he had not meant to jump down his throat.

"Well you'd best get back to your father's, it won't be long till we start eating."

And as he said it, he began to smell the food in the air. The feast that had been meant for him the other day was now surely going ahead.

Walking back to his father's, he opened the door and walked in to find his father alone. His father's gaze was wandering the floor, in deep thought.

But he looked up as his shadow broke into the room.

"Sorry…I was thinking about your mother."

He sat down next to him. The fire was still going beside them.

"What was she like?"

His father's eyes seemed to hold the sadness he could never have seen.

"She was beautiful, I never felt complete without her. I remember the day we met, I had been walking outside the castle by myself, and I was a little older than you are now. She had been kneeling beside the road picking the red bellflowers, she looked so beautiful I didn't even realise the Storm raging behind. The flowers she was picking only grew close to the edge of the Acias, it was something in the way that the air moved that made them grow only there."

He paused, collecting his thoughts.

"I told her she should be inside where it was safe, but she just told me she was fine, acting completely oblivious to the fact that the Storm was so close. I told her something so beautiful should not be so close to something of such ferocity. She laughed and said, "If I were a flower as beautiful as this, then would you take me away from the Storm?"

For a moment I didn't know what to say, but then I replied as best I could. I said that I would protect her from the Storm and not take her away."

His father had been smiling whilst looking towards the floor away from him and Graciou could see he still loved his mother deeply. Graciou hoped he might one day remember something of who she was.

"I never knew."

His father paused before replying, taking in the memory once more.

"I know, there are so many things like that I have not been able to tell you. I hope in time I will."

He was sure some sort of meat could be smelt wafting inward through the doors.

"We're going to be late for the feast, I think it's starting."

His father got up from his chair and walked over to the bedroom, speaking as he went.

"Yes, it's good you reminded me, I had nearly forgotten about it. Did you get to see the eating area before with Sophia?"

He had not thought of her for at least an hour, but strangely he felt like he wanted to be with her nonetheless.

"I saw it, she showed me the tables."

His father had expected him to say more and prompted him.

"And?"

"Well, that was it really."

He walked over to get his new clothes for the evening, which looked a lot smarter than what he had been wearing.

"It's good to see the two of you getting to know each other."

Able to tell that his father was trying to, in all the best ways, find out what they had spoken about, he smiled to himself, changing into his clothes quickly.

His father was at the door ready for him, as they both exited out onto the staircase below.

The eating area was full of people, most of which he did not know, his father walked in from behind him. Barnabe was already seated at the high table. His father sat down at the table that had been placed higher than most of the others. He did not yet see anyone he knew, and was a little unnerved by the crowd that surrounded him and his father. Barnabe came in and sat opposite him, with his back to most of the crowded tables behind.

"Good evening Graciou."

"Evening, Barnabe."

He said it as if they had never been apart from each other, not in all those thirteen years. The Captain entered next and his father stood, waving them over to the table.

"Kurubin, please come and sit with us; your men too."

Each of them stood and walked up to the high table, the Captain sitting beside Barnabe on his right and the other men filling in the other seats.

"I can't thank you all enough for bringing Graciou back to us," Barnabe said to the captain and his men.

"Indeed, if Graciou had not found us, we might still be at a loss."

One of the servants had walked in from a concealed entrance behind the high table with a tray of wine and other drinks, which were deposited on all the crowded tables below.

"How is your arm feeling Kurubin?"

He put his glass down on the table and looked over in his direction.

"Much better, thank you, I just had to sleep off the effects."

"Glad to hear you're feeling better. That figure has to have been one of the most vile in temperament that I have ever seen."

His father brought it up as if the experience had been an every-day occurrence, so deeply engrained into all of them, that it did not matter.

"Indeed it was, I've never seen one so violent before, nor so keen on taking one so young."

"Well, if its origins are anything to go by, then it is understandable."

Kurubin frowned, neither his father nor Barnabe asked him what he meant.

"How so Graciou?"

The Storms of Acias

"Well, the figure came from the Storm itself, I ascertained that whilst I was in the town."

Each of them looked shocked as he said it.

"So they did come from the Storm, so many people have been wondering about that for so long…"

His father smiled tensely, it was not an easy smile, it revealed his eagerness not to discuss the point.

"It would appear so."

Graciou knew however, that the figure had left a trail of mysterious events behind it that he himself had not yet managed to unravel. One thing he was sure of was the figure's ability to hurt whomever it got close to.

As the evening continued, more wine was poured and several courses of food were consumed. Hours later the noise and chatter had died down and everyone appeared to be full and rather jolly.

Various jokes and laughter passed around the table, but wherever he looked he could not find Sophia anywhere on any of the tables; he turned to his father.

"Is Sophia not eating with us tonight?"

He looked around at him.

"She should be, isn't she here?"

"Well I can't see her."

He gave the room another look.

"Strange, you should probably go check if she's coming down or not."

He got up from the table and excused himself for however long it would take.

As he got to the house, her door was ajar as he walked in, which should have meant she was just inside. But as he peered into the room, he couldn't see her, on the bed or by the washbasin. She didn't appear to be in the other slightly smaller room either. But then as he turned back towards the door he saw something catch out of the corner of his eye; it was some sort of wooden plate grafted over the wall.

Toying with the mechanism that was obviously attached to it he tried to pull whatever it was away. No sooner had he done it than a blast of cold and icy wind blew into him, knocking all the warmth out of him. Grabbing the coat that must have been hers, he crouched and scrambled through the low opening, to find himself in some sort of passageway, it was freezing and he could see snow had settled on the floor. But there appeared to be no ice.

Then at the far end of the corridor, where it jutted out at a sharp angle, he could see someone. They darted away from him and he got up to run after them. He caught them a few seconds later and as he did so they turned around to face him. Catching Sophia's arms as she began to fall sideways, he saw it was her.

"Graciou?"

Why had she been running from him he wondered?

"Yes it's me, what are you doing out here?"

She tried to look away from him, but his arms were still holding hers.

"I come here sometimes, the cold air makes me feel better."

She had been turning to look out the rough open slit for a window, but he pulled her back toward him.

"You shouldn't be out here, what if one of those things…"

He stopped, for he knew that she didn't have any idea what they were.

"What things?" she enquired.

"It doesn't matter."

"No Graciou, it matters."

She was adamant to get it out of him.

"It was something in the town that's all, I attacked it and it vanished. Once I got back to the castle my father figured that it might have followed me here. Which it had."

"And it's still here?"

As suddenly as they had entered into conversation about it, from the end of the other corridor, he saw something, it was dark, but he could make it out nonetheless. Something was there, gesturing for him to come closer to it, as if trying to coax him forward.

"What's wrong, Graciou?"

His gaze broke as he looked down at her, her gaze quickly looking back down the corridor to where it was stood, but instead she merely looked back up at him.

"Was something there?"

As he looked again, the form had gone from his view.

"No…No it's gone."

"What were you thinking about?"

"Something I've seen before, but it doesn't matter."

He could not understand what it was he had seen, it could have been a figure, but it did not look quite like one and had made no move toward him.

But still it was strange that he should see something like that. Getting back to Sophia he took off the coat he had on, placing it over her shoulders.

"Have you eaten?" he said as they stood there.

"Not yet."

"Come on then, there's still plenty of food left I'm sure."

He put his arm around her shoulder and lead her back to the opening from which he had come. They both moved through the narrow gap, which he fastened shut behind him, rubbing his arms for warmth.

He waited outside for her to change, as she came back out to eat. She was wearing a long dress which waved around her ankles and had put her hair up slightly.

"You look amazing..."

He had said it without being prompted, for she did indeed look amazing. Smiling in reply they both walked down to the dining area.

When they got back down the room was scattered with a few people, talking and conversing. Some turned to look at them, but most just carried on with their conversations.

"I best sit over here then."

She looked up at him, as if waiting for something. But he knew his father wouldn't mind.

"My father won't mind, sit with us. If you want to of course."

"I'd love to."

She smiled and waited for him to take the lead, as they both walked up to the large high table. His father stood up, even if he had trouble doing so, to welcome them both to the table.

"Ahh, I was wondering where you two had got to. Where did you find her Graciou?"

There was a short flicker of apprehension in her eyes and then he spoke.

"Just appears Sophia forgot the feast was on."

It was a slightly feeble excuse, which he doubted his father would not have known.

"Strange, we gave everyone notice. But it's no matter, please sit with us both of you."

They sat down beside each other at the other end of the table.

"I was just about to talk to the Captain about what we discussed earlier."

Nodding he noticed that Sophia had begun to add to her plate.

"On top of the toast we made earlier, I would like to make one now, to the health and wellbeing of Graciou."

His father had surely been drinking, for he startled everyone as he raised his glass. Each of the others did the same and each toasted to his good health.

"I would also like to toast to the health and wellbeing of all and hope that we will continue to be so for a long time to come."

He raised his glass, as the others stood, but both him and Sophia remained seated. Their glasses tinkled together, and he watched each of them take a drink and sit back down again. He remembered that Barnabe had told him earlier, that he should find out more about the properties of the cross and seeing as he had the wealth of knowledge right next to him, he saw no reason not to ask about it.

Turning to Kurubin he began to speak.

"Barnabe was telling me earlier that Sophia and I should look up the properties of the cross. Seeing as I'm sure we'd both rather hear it from you, how do they work?"

The Captain turned to him and lifted the cross that he was wearing from his head, placing it onto the table face down.

"Each of us has one of these crosses, they look to most outsiders like a piece of carved wood, but to each and every one of us they are special. We each go through a ceremony, which you are both building up to, where these crosses are handed to you."

"So they are handed to us as a sort of rite of passage?"

He tried to understand the Captain's words.

"Yes, but more than that, depending on the engraving on the back they each hold power within. Only the person who carries the cross knows of it's power and only that person can find out what it is capable of."

"Each specific to it's wearer?"

Sophia said from beside him.

"Correct, I know what mine is capable of, but you have to wonder what else it can do, because each cross is the same, only the ceremony and the words define its power. Take Mr and Mrs Grentshaw for example," as he said the words he saw Sophia look away for a second, but he also noticed she was clutching the locket at her chest. "The crosses that the both of them used were able to control the violently erratic nature of the Acias itself."

Kurubin paused taking a drink from his glass.

"What makes them so powerful?" Graciou asked.

"The wearer alone gives it power, beyond that, it is useless. Though you will notice the reverse has a compass attached, which will always point to a place of safety."

Graciou remembered now when he had used the cross and how it had guided him to various places, now able to see that it was either pointing him towards a place of safety, or away from another concealed or ever present danger.

"Yes, I have used it."

"You have used the crosses of others?"

Kurubin seemed interested to hear how he had managed it.

"To come here I used them, but only as a means of direction."

"Ahh, I thought you meant you had used them freely. That would indeed be interesting."

He smiled, returning the same smile to Sophia.

"Barnabe, when do you think we will be ready for the ceremony?"

"If Kurubin has told you all you need to know, then you are ready, if you feel you are both ready for it, you can take the ceremony tomorrow."

"I guess we are," he said, looking over at Sophia.

"I wish we knew more, but I guess we'll learn that afterwards."

The Captain spoke.

"Indeed you will, it all comes with practice, you will become better as time passes."

16

The dinner finished with him and his father bidding goodnight to those who remained, telling Sophia that he would see her tomorrow. She smiled, saying she looked forward to it and they both began walking back up to his father's quarters.

"Do you feel ready for this son?" his father had asked, whilst they had been walking. Graciou looked up at him, as if he weren't making any sense.

"I guess so, if you…"

"No, do you feel ready for this, it's not up to me anymore."

"I'm ready."

He had said it without really questioning or thinking, but he wanted to show his father what he could do.

The next day came without pause and his father was already awake beside the fire when he woke. They both left from the house and walked toward Sophia's, meeting with her as his father lead them up a new set of steps, which he had not seen before. Sophia herself looked smartly dressed and pretty, she had obviously taken extra attention at looking good for the ceremony that was going to take place.

He had dressed as formally as he could, as it appeared this would be the most formal thing he had done since he had been back. The steps were steep and it took them a good while to walk up them, as they spiralled round toward the chandelier in the ceiling.

"Sophia, you should wait here with Kurubin. I'll be back to fetch you up there later on," his father said, as they had walked past some sort of side room in the wall. Sophia nodded as he said it, "Good luck Graciou."

"Thanks," he said, smiling at her as they returned to climbing the last few steps towards the open room above.

The room patterned out like a sort of flat disk, with no apparent walls. There was a kind of flat rough stone at the back of it and the chandelier cut into the side of it, the larger half of the disk leaning over the citadel below. His father stopped at the doorway.

"Go over to those two men, I'll be here once you're done."

The Storms of Acias

His father gave him a look of reassurance as he patted his shoulder for luck. Slowly he turned, walking over to them, feeling more apprehensive with every step. The men were wearing red robes, each matching each other in near perfection. Whoever these men were he had never seen them before. His stomach felt sick, unsure of what might be ahead of him.

"We the prophets, who have brought your name through so many generations, have been bestowed the power to grant the ceremony of Gracious. With this we will ask of you several questions, answer each as they come. Are you ready to take the ceremony trial Graciou? From here on in you won't be able to go back, if you do so, the ceremony will become void."

Their words sounded harsh, but given the meaning of the ceremony, he guessed it was worthy of such dramatic words.

"Turn to face the cross that has been laid out in the glass altar."

Where the flat floor cut into the chandelier, a glass altar of sorts was resting, which had sunken into it the wooden cross he would receive.

"Graciou, I would like you to move forward and place one hand over the cross. Do not touch the cross or glass. Merely place your palm over the cross and state these words:

"I Graciou, Excemaratis, Gracious, swear to give my life in the preservation of one so great and I swear to preserve thy power before me."

He re-iterated the words as he placed his palm over the cross, calming now as he started to relax. Following their words was not so bad after all.

But his hand seemed fixed to the spot as he tried to lift it back to his side. A weird sensation had taken over it, making it stiff, as if his very bones were fused together.

An intense heat began to rise from below, turning slowly to more of a burning sensation; desperately he tried to hold it back, for he did not want to void the ceremony.

"Graciou, I would now like you to pick up the cross from the glass."

Slowly, he moved his hand to the glass, and suddenly some form of movement returned to it. But the heat still persisted and as he picked it up, he could feel the same heat from it's wooden surface.

"Now place the cross over your head."

Still holding the cross in one hand, he placed the leather string over his head. But as he did so the room began to blur around him, the white colours merged in and out of each other. Suddenly, he felt extremely sick, his entire body dizzy and uncontrollable, as he began to fall backwards. In front of him stood someone he had not seen before, his face was blurry with his current vision, but nonetheless he knew it was a familiar face.

Slowly he moved up from the floor with great difficulty, feeling as if a gigantic weight had been pressed onto his entire body.

"Graciou, I come with a message for you and you alone, it is very important you listen to me."

It's voice was familiar; it sounded like he knew the voice itself, but couldn't place it.

"Who are you?"

Graciou forced his tired lungs to breath, now trying hard to concentrate on what was in front of him. Gently his body started to go numb all over, the weight lifting from it as if it had never been there.

His father's face came into view, crouching close by him.

"Back away from him Excem!" he heard a prophet shout over at what had to have been his father.

"Graciou? Graciou?!"

His father's voice was at a shout; looking extremely frightened for his life, Kurubin behind him.

"Sir what's..."

"Graciou, what's wrong?"

But he was not listening, the cross lay a few metres from his feet, crawling forward he picked it up, able to feel the warmth of it in his hands.

"This will never be allowed to go ahead!" shouted one of the prophets from behind him.

"Silence!" his father shouted in their direction, obviously not willing to take on board what they had said.

Placing it over his head, he gently let it fall onto his bare chest. For a minute he felt nothing, but then a sudden and violent force overtook him, throwing him backward into the air, as he smacked into the back wall of the room. The cross had been ripped from his neck, now floating just in front of the glass altar. The two leather ends floated around in the air contradicting reality itself.

A tremendous white light illuminated from somewhere up ahead as he watched, tearing the wooden cross asunder. His mind was spinning wildly as he tried to regain a sense of himself, searching around the room for something to fix onto, his father soon came running over to him.

"GRACIOU!"

The prophets looked disgusted from the other side of the room, but with his current vision he was unsure what they were feeling. Two more men walked in to help his father, their faces pale and worried. Gently they lifted him up from the floor, taking him out towards the doorway as they did so, but just as he crossed the entrance to the room his body fell limp, exhausted and unable to carry on.

He woke in his bed, the room was quiet and the light had been dimmed, no one appeared to be sat around the chairs at the fireplace, Sophia was sat beside his bed. It appeared she had been for quite some time. He looked at her as she smiled, but his mind was pressed with questions, what had happened to him? Had he completed the ceremony? Or was he having some sort of dream?

"How long have you been here?" he asked her, bluntly.

"A few hours, your father brought you back in here, we were all pretty worried. I should really go and tell him that you're awake."

She looked pleased that he hadn't been hurt, though his head was pulsing rapidly. Turning in the bed he felt the sheets catching on his chest and in near agony he pulled them away, staring down as he looked at the searing scar below, each piece of it appearing to have the words that were on the cross he had used. Sophia put a hand to it obviously aware it hurt.

"When did that happen?"

"A few days ago, it was nothing."

He didn't want to make her too aware of the figure, if he could help it. She took her hand out of his and walked over to the other side of the bed for the bandage he had left, which was still clean enough to be used.

In obvious discomfort he replied.

"It was when that thing attacked me, my father told me to grab the cross, in fright I pulled it against my chest and I could feel it burning into my skin." She looked astonished, for she had never heard of a cross harming someone.

"The cross did this to you?"

"Yes, but it's weird, it healed so quickly. I can see it now just after the ceremony and yet I haven't been able to see it for the past two days or more."

"What happened up there anyway?" she said looking worried, with no obvious idea what had gone on.

"I'm still not sure, I do know that I saw something though, it was so familiar."

She looked up as she was putting the bandage around his side.

"What did it look like?"

"It was dressed in dark clothes and it's face looked like someone I knew, but my vision was so fuzzy, I couldn't get a decent view of it."

Not wanting to mention that it had spoken to him, he stopped, pausing for thought whilst she took in what he had said.

"Well, I better go and tell him you're awake."

For a moment, as she got up, he wondered if she thought him mad, but as she left, he instinctively knew this was not the case.

Ever since he had got back and begun unravelling his past, it appeared all he had done was uncover even greater and more prominent mysteries and secrets. His heritage was becoming larger and more impressive by the day and gradually it was beginning to feel like it was not even real.

The minutes ticked on by as he waited, but no-one appeared in the room and he continued to think.

What if someone had got hurt? Someone else he had not seen at the time? And then what of the cross? Staring at the window he looked at it, wishing he had more answers to more questions than he did currently. But as he looked a very strange thing happened, for the glass changed to a light blue tint and from the other side a cascading light shone through, bouncing rainbow-like rays into the room. Unable to understand what was going on he stared at it, the sight of it fixing his mind in place, turning back to see something standing at the foot of his bed and he jumped with fright.

The person seemed fixed to the spot, tranced, lifeless in it's expression.

"Who are you stranger?"

It's eyes were fixed on the headboard behind him and stayed in the same place as it spoke, softly, and yet he felt, with experience beyond his own.

"My name is not important."

He stared at it, still completely transfixed by it's speech.

"Why have you appeared here then?"

"You sent for me."

His heart began to pick up, their beats interlacing, wondering exactly who this person was and how he could have possibly sent for them.

"I don't remember doing so."

It didn't answer, obviously it had not come to speak out of context.

"Why did I call you?"

"You called because you wanted answers."

It was as if the thing was reading his thoughts, as if it knew what he had been thinking all along. So he asked the most prevalent question that was currently on his mind.

"What happened earlier?"

"Right now your father is conversing with the entire council, because the prophecy that they have laid faith in for longer than they can remember, has just come true. But right now those same people are disbelieving that you are even who you appear to be. Some say that you are another figure come to harm them, others that the prophecy holds no weight anymore."

As it sunk in, he started to see it forming in front of him, his father and several others, all conversing about him. He wondered exactly what would become of it.

"But what of the ceremony?"

"When you participated in the ceremony, there was an extreme and violent reaction, one that permeates through time itself. They tried to place a hallowed name upon an item. Which could not bear it's weight. Neither the wood nor yourself could bear such a transition. Your father and others were apprehensive in the last few days, because they were not sure what would happen, some of those same people now think themselves fools for letting you try."

His mind spun, as if finally he had got all the answers he had wanted since he had come here, no less from a ghost at the end of his bed.

"What should I do?"

"Once they have come to a decision about you, as well as that of the prophecy, they will come to find you, or to exile you from this place. Whether you choose to act as if this has given you a new second sight, or that you remain as you were before the ceremony, is up to you. Whatever you choose you have those choices and more. But I would advise you to choose wisely."

It's stern voice paused again, it was like having your mind pulled from your very head and then let go of again. What should he do? Tell them that it had all been for nothing? Face exile and lose all he had gained? One thing was for sure, Sophia would now be speaking with his father and the others and they would be on their way here.

"How long do I have?"

But the ghost had already disappeared from his view. He searched about the room, but it had vanished.

Minutes later the door flew open, several men stepping into the room, each looking up toward his direction. The look of his father's anger filled the room, though kept at bay, he saw it none the less and he could tell that whatever they had been speaking of, it had taken a long time to come to any sort of decision. Something about his father told him, no matter what had been said and no matter how much talking took place, these men would not have backed down from their opinions. One of them stepped forward to speak, his long drawn out voice was cold and emotionless.

"Graciou Excemaratis, it has been proposed by the council of the highest of elders, to choose for you your fate in what we have discussed. Due to the extreme way in which you reacted at the ceremony, many of us are unsure whether to consider you as friend or foe. We wish to ask of you one question that we have each agreed must be asked."

He paused, as if waiting for something. Barnabe stood in at the back of the group, looking daunted and yet composed.

"So we come to ask. After you took the ceremony, have you come to see a difference in yourself, is your mind and body deformed in ways that it was not before? Or do you believe you have come out of it no different?"

He stared at him, not speaking, making sure he felt the way in which he was being disrespected. Opening his mouth, he spoke, giving no doubt in anyone's mind as to his now blatant anger.

"I was of the mind that my father embraced me as his own."

They looked at each other, answering back quickly.

"That is correct."

"Then why do you think that I could be anything less than I am? If my father saw me as the son he thought he might have lost, then what right do you have to doubt him?"

One of the men, slightly off centre to the speaker, turned to give his father a long and silent interpretation of his words.

"I would please ask that you answer the question we have given you to answer and converse on other topics with us no more."

His tone was cold and obvious, as if he had come to the finer edge of his patience. He thought it over quickly.

"I will not answer the question in the way that you would wish, for I myself have an interpretation on it. That is, that I am of a new mind, one that parallels that of my previous one, but this mind knows more than my last."

His rage was still building and he was troubled with holding it back, but it appeared he had gotten his message across. His father's face appeared to brighten as he had said it. The man to the centre looked embarrassed and abashed and turned around to the others, before returning to face him.

"We will have to discuss your reply," he said hurriedly, "for we must make sure we are right in the matter."

But before he had a chance to turn his back, he answered him back.

"I hope you find right, in the same way that you find faith."

The old man turned back to answer, his face red and angry, he could tell he had hit the only true thing in each of their lives. Quickly, he turned on his heel, marching out of the room, the other men trailing behind him. As they walked out, his father looked up at him out of the corner of his eye, giving him an inconspicuous wink.

17

The day drew on, his mind continuing to think on the events of earlier and wondering what would come of them. He knew he had made an impression and it seemed his father had felt it the right one. Barnabe had not conversed with him, not giving anything away as usual. The fire crackled away slowly as he watched it, starting to cool and turn into grey ash, resembling the lingering thoughts of his now bored mind.

He woke to find he had not slept long. The fire was now completely out and the light from the window had now dimmed sufficiently, the small lights the only illumination around him. There had been no interruption of his sleep and his mind worried over what might have come from their talking.

They had no right to speak to him in the way they did and he doubted his father approved of what they had said or done. It had been hours before they had spoken with him; he guessed that the deliberation among them was carrying on longer than they thought it would and the conversation was becoming more heated by the moment.

Just as his mind was turning to the fact they might indeed have given up all together, the door edged ajar and stopped, no one entered. As he sat there wondering who it might be, he could see the presence of many people outside, each talking to each other and looking towards the hovel. Someone was stood in the doorway, but it was still too far forward to see him or her.

Once the talk outside had died down, his Uncle came into view, looking quite happy with himself, closing the doorway behind him. He walked over to the chair without looking up at him and gave him a smile; he knew now everything was all-right.

"What did they say?"

Barnabe was jubilant, as he should have been, but more jubilant than usual.

"I heard what you said, from your own father's lips, you couldn't have answered any better. They decided that they were mistaken about your dramatic exit from the ceremony and that we had been in the right. Your father was angry with them as soon as they suggested what you might be. He carried you out of there faster than anything. Those elder prophets are so sceptical, they really will jump to any conclusion."

He stopped, looking over him with a proud sense of achievement.

"They say that they do speak for you and the prophecy, but really they just speak for themselves."

Barnabe stopped, looking disgruntled but still pleased that it was over. He could see now the faith both Barnabe and his father had held onto for so long, and all the agonising that went along with it, had lifted from their minds.

"What were they saying outside?"

"The prophets made an announcement earlier to everyone, squashing any rumours; letting everyone know the prophecy had come true. None of them wanted to, but your father made them say it. Everyone's intrigued with the story; they wanted to know what was happening. It was their right after all."

He nodded.

"I'm a rising star now then?" Graciou said sarcastically.

Barnabe laughed.

"It would appear so, most of the Citadel is alive with talk of you. Most can't believe it."

"It must be a relief for them, to finally see that it's come true."

"Indeed it must, but…"

Barnabe stopped, his face becoming more serious about the matter.

"How do you feel about it all?"

He would never have expected Barnabe to speak to him the way he was now, for it had never been Barnabe's character to do so. But as the words sank in, he did indeed feel uneasy about what had gone on: the fact that people were so quick to persecute him.

"I guess I don't want to let them down, now they know it's come true. Part of me still doesn't see why I'm so special."

Barnabe's face did not falter, keeping the same serious composure.

"Yes, I must admit, I wouldn't completely believe it myself," Barnabe paused, turning back from the fireplace.

"But don't mind it?"

"Its fine."

Graciou said it more to re-assure him than anything else, it was something he didn't want his Uncle of all people to be worrying about.

"You know that night? What was it you were shouting about?"

Barnabe looked as if he didn't want to speak of it, but circumstances had since changed.

"Nothing much, we just talked about the prophecy, I wasn't sure…if you were really coming true. Your father was still bent on not telling you anything of it, he still wanted to shield you from what it entailed. The nurse, who is a very good friend of your father's, wasn't too pleased with his attitude. She knew more than us that you needed to know."

Graciou smiled.

"It was as if you were in on what we were saying earlier, the way you spoke."

He looked up, his face trying to hide what had really happened, but Barnabe was already watching him.

"You knew?"

Barnabe spoke still probing his answer.

"I er…"

Barnabe moved in closer.

"Whatever it is, you have to tell me."

Of all the people that he would have lied to, Barnabe had to be the worst when it came to confrontation.

"It was when I woke up, after Sophia had left, I was still in bed. I'd been staring into the window beside me and wishing I knew what was going on."

He gulped, hoping Barnabe wouldn't freak out once he had told him about it.

"I asked it questions, it replied with what I needed to know, no doubt in it's voice."

Barnabe looked up, an empathetic grin on his face, looking over to the window as he got up from his chair.

"There's a reason why Graciou, one that doesn't border on insanity."

Barnabe smiled briefly, crouching beside one of the windows.

"Most people think the bodies of those that died all those years ago, were left to freeze or rot in the fields and on the roads. But some we managed to give a decent burial, we buried them in the way we have always buried our own."

He picked up his cross and glided it across the bottom of the window, a panel flew to the side and a buffed gold plaque stared back at them. The name "Richard, Stockswell, Excemaratis" roughly etched into its surface.

Graciou got up, walking over to it, eyes fixed firmly on the plaque, then turning his eyes to meet Barnabe's.

"He's buried in there?"

"Yes, they were all buried in box coffins, most we managed to retrieve, those who are old enough still remember. But don't you see what's happened?"

He stared at him, he himself thought he knew, but he was still trying to grapple with it.

"Somehow, and I have no idea how it is possible, it must have been Stockswell who appeared at the foot of your bed."

Barnabe spoke as if there was no questioning it. That had to be the cause of the appearance and he knew it was the most likely cause.

"It doesn't make any sense Barnabe."

Eyes skimming over the carpeted floor below him, a cold sweat seeped into his mind and body. Indeed, it felt as if he had been punched, for if what was being said was true and it could hardly be anything less. What was happening to him?

His Uncle walked back over to the chair by the fire, sitting down into it and taking a pipe out from his pocket.

"I don't often smoke, we don't have enough of the stuff to go around anymore."

He lit the pipe and put his feet up, resting his neck on the back of the chair.

"I can't believe…how…I can see ghosts now?"

Barnabe laughed for a second, then turning slightly more serious.

"The prophecy stated you would be able to do some things that others could not do. That I believe, may well be one of them."

He was sure that Barnabe would keep what had happened between them a secret.

"But surely my father will find out?"

He turned to him once more.

"Don't worry, he won't think badly of it. As long as we keep it between us, I don't suspect he shall know."

Slowly, more secrets were unveiling from inside this cold fortress. It was as if he had been the catalyst and he was at the edge of the explosive rift, hurtling at massive speed, toward the destruction of a foundation so firm and yet his sights were already fixed on the wreckage behind. Barnabe had been looking at him, trying to get some sense out of his confused gaze.

"What is it Graciou?"

He looked up, shaking himself out of it.

"So much is happening so fast, I feel as if I'm spinning out of control."
Barnabe smiled.

"It can often seem that way Graciou, more so I imagine for you right
now than for anyone else here." Barnabe paused, as if looking for the words
to best comfort him. "But we each learn to deal with it differently, we each
do just that, we learn to deal with it. Eventually you will do so as well."

He smiled at him, knowing that what had been said was meant for the
best. Relaxed by his words he reclined back in the chair, Barnabe gently
puffing on his pipe as he sat next to him.

As the hours drew on, the afternoon light that filtered mysteriously in
from the window faded to a dark orange glow, as his father walked in late
that evening. Walking over to him he placed a hand down onto his shoulder, patting it once before moving away to get a drink.

"I've spoken with the others, they seem to have got the message about
you now."

"You've been gone a long time, must have been hard work."
Excemaratis smiled.

"Well they won't try to be so rash and blunt with their thoughts and
actions in the future. I'm sorry you had to go through that."

Graciou smiled at him.

"It can't be helped."

"No, but they should know better. How long has Barnabe been
asleep?"

And indeed he was asleep, his pipe had fallen to the floor from his hand
and his face was stern but resolute as he slept.

"I hadn't noticed."

"Yes, well I guess we've all been preoccupied."

"I'm sure Barnabe will tell you what we talked about, I think I will get
some rest." Graciou said, moving over toward the other room.

Excem smiled at him once more.

"You know I'm proud of what you did today, don't you?"

He nodded, he had been unsure earlier what his father had been thinking, so many things at once it seemed.

"Sleep well son." He heard his father whisper as he sat down into the
chair, next to a stirring Barnabe.

"I will," he spoke back, as sleep dragged him down once more, onto the mountainous plains of his dreams.

His eyes opened wide and fast, the room exploding into view as he woke. Barnabe was sat next to him and his father was asleep in the bed. He got up, stretching as he did so. A quiet knock issued from the door and quickly checking both of them were still asleep, he walked over to it. Sophia was there, dressed in new clothes and looking somewhat older than when he had last seen her. He could see people walking past looking up at them both. Taking her by the shoulder he led her in.

She was quick to talk, as if she had been desperate to do so since yesterday.

"I heard about what happened, for a while I wasn't sure what was going on, they say you're the Graciou everyone's been waiting for."

Her eyes caught Barnabe who shuffled in the chair and his father asleep in the bed. She brought her voice to a slight whisper as she carried on.

"You know I was quite worried about you, I wasn't sure whether you'd wake up or not."

She pulled in closer to him.

"Well it was nice to see your face when I woke."

He tried to say it without showing his nerves, but instead she merely put a hand to his chest and kissed him gently. She pulled away once more, sitting down in the chair by the fire. Partially stunned by the move, he moved forward to where the two chairs sat. His uncle woke up suddenly, with a slight snort, looking around at them wearily.

"It's morning I take it?" he said wincing.

"It's morning. Sophia has just got here."

He turned to look at her, overseeing her, then moved back in the chair.

"Well, there's a lot that we must do for the both of you today and I have been told to take over the proceedings for that."

They both looked at him, Sophia spoke first.

"How do you mean?"

"Well, seeing as you've got your cross we better show you how to use it."

He could see the leather strap now cradled around her neck, turning to him she replied.

"But what about Graciou?"

"Graciou should watch, so he knows how it works. Even though he may not have a cross, it's still a skill he should learn."

She did not look as if she disagreed with him, but he was Barnabe and she was not about to disagree.

"I think we should leave while your father's still asleep."

He lifted the blanket that had been over him and laid it beside the chair, trying to pat the creases out of his clothes. Walking toward the doorway he turned around to face them.

"If you'll both follow me, Graciou you can watch from the side, I'll show Sophia what to do."

They both stepped out of the door with him, shutting it behind them, Graciou walking alongside Sophia. He found it funny how Barnabe was instantly attentive. Then again when he had been back in the town, with the high probability of the Storm appearing at any time, he had to be.

"Did you try the short exercise I gave you last night?"

Obviously Barnabe had already spoken with Sophia about today's proceedings, but he did not mind.

"Yes, it was amazing, I'd never felt anything like it before. That place you told me to search for was incredible."

"Good, you'll use it today to do various things with the cross."

They had entered a short passageway, just at the top of the marble staircase, which was a complete dead end. "Now this will look like any other ordinary corridor to both of you I'm sure. Graciou on the other hand, might remember it differently. Watch closely Sophia."

Graciou had no idea why Barnabe thought he should, but he did feel as if this had been the way they had come in. It didn't look anything like it had then.

Barnabe took the cross out from his chest and held it out toward the wall. Without any noise or effect, a segment of it became translucent, and he instantly recognised it as the doorway to and from the chambers at the front of the citadel. It was very strange, for when they had walked toward it, he had felt as if it was just a wall, like his mind had blanked out the memory of his entrance, forcing him to forget.

"Follow me."

Barnabe walked forward and so did they, the thick translucent wall feeling as cold as it had the first time he had walked through it.

"This is what we call the Arrival Hall."

Sophia looked around, interested at everything she saw.

"I have memories of this place, but I don't remember ever being here."

"That's because once we left the town in the valley floor, we took everyone through here. The fortress itself was built at least three hundred years ago by Excemaratis the second. He issued the orders for it to be built."

His eyes fixed on Graciou, confirming to him that the fortress was built out of fear and not for any other reason.

"I see, so when would we use it?"

Her obvious knowledge of the reason behind the need for its construction showed.

"In case we were attacked, we would all come through here and into the two chambers that proceed these two. There, we would fight."

"But why would we ever need to fight?" she said laughing.

"Well if ever we got attacked by the storm, with more numbers than we could cope with, we would come here."

He paused and then continued.

"You saw me open the doorway just before?"

"Yes, why?" she said inquisitively.

"It took me a great amount of time to learn, but I opened that doorway by using the same place I told you to search for the other evening."

Unsure what exactly it was had been said, Graciou butted in.

"What exactly is the place you're talking about?"

Barnabe looked over at him, aware that he should have told him before.

"Sorry, Graciou. I was telling Sophia last night, it's a state of mind, which if used in conjunction with the cross, unlocks the power of our mind."

"How is it possible for you to do that, using the place you speak of?" Sophia said.

"When I concentrate on the image of it, I am able to project that from myself through my body and into the cross in my hand. But do not be fooled into thinking that the cross holds any power, for beyond it's shape it is nothing more than a piece of wood. It is our minds that do the work. I am able to open and close the passage at will, but it takes a great deal of time, as I said earlier, to learn. Some things are much easier to learn than others."

Sophia had picked up her cross and was staring at the back of it.

"What's this glass ball for?"

Barnabe stepped forward to her.

"Each cross has a small glass hollow globe built into it. You can see the pin underneath, that points in various directions. If the bearer is the right person it will point towards a place of safety, a place such as the fortress. If not, it will point toward that of an unsafe place it's a form of dissuasion that's built into the globe itself. That way no-one can find us who shouldn't be able to."

So now he knew why the various lines on the globe had spun around the way they had. But on the cross that he had been given by Marcus, a red line had been etched into it. Nowhere on either Sophia or Barnabe's cross could he find such an etching, and as his journey had been so strange, guiding him in the end not to a place of safety, but of danger…he did wonder.

"So, what's next?" Sophia had said.

She looked over at him and gave him a smile. He smiled back and returned his eyes to watching them both.

"I think I will teach you how to defend yourself. It's one of the easiest things to learn and something you will have never done before. I will be the one attacking you, but the defence you shall use against me will be projected from your mind."

He moved back, against one of the walls near the hearth.

"One more thing, you must make sure never to take any of the passages to my left or right. These passages are pits that stretch for hundreds of thousands of feet into the mountain base, they are there in case anyone ever managed to breach the chambers."

She nodded and so did Graciou. He had wondered exactly what they were for, now he knew.

"When I begin to run at you, I will unsheathe my sword, but I will not harm you. Once I am within a few feet, grab your cross and hold it against your chest, but make sure that you are thinking of the same place I taught you."

Barnabe began to run toward her, his sword high in the air, coming down low, swinging madly out to the right and then stopping dead barely inches from her face.

"Why didn't you take out your cross?" Barnabe said, a patient but slightly angered tone in his voice. She looked stunned and slightly frightened.

"Err, I was waiting like you told me to, you were so fast."

His anger subsided and he took his place once more.

"Never mind, this time remember to take the cross out from your chest, if you don't wish to wait, you don't have to."

Again, he picked up pace and again his sword swung out to the right, dropping in toward her face, but this time she pulled the cross from her chest. As Barnabe's sword came crashing down toward her, a blinding flash of iridescent white light lit up the room around where she had drawn the cross, throwing Barnabe's sword out from his hand, shattering it into a thousand pieces as it did so.

"Oh GOD!" she cried as the incandescent light illuminated the corridor.

Barnabe was a few feet away, lying flat out on his back. Slowly he tried to pick himself up, his arm still holding the end of the blade. He walked forward to her, with a look not of confusing as he might of expected, but what appeared to be astonishment.

"Can you swear to me, that you have never done this before?"

Graciou had already walked forward to help her stand and she slowly began to answer.

"No, never Barnabe."

"Never before?" Barnabe re-iterated the question, his disbelief evident in his voice.

"Never."

"I have never seen such a shield as impressive as that. Not since..." his voice trailed off, as if he knew of only one.

"Since when?" Graciou asked.

"Not since your father was first attacked."

"Was it the storm?"

"No. It was when your father was younger, he ran into a figure in the grounds near the castle. It was fast, quickly trying to turn his mind against him, stopping him from being able to defend himself. But somehow he managed to break free of it, grabbing his cross and all at once the biggest shield I've ever seen lit up the air around him, the figure phased out of the very air for a few seconds, staggering backwards toward me. I stood there unable to believe my eyes."

He stopped. Sophia looked scared at the very idea of it being true. Graciou now had an inkling about why Barnabe had always seemed to be in the shadow of his father. Barnabe carried on.

"You see, the reasons we have all of these safeguards aren't just for show. Out there are real dangers, without this," he touched his cross, "we are lost completely."

He felt the spot where his cross should have lain, his smile returning slowly, shading the certainty of his face from view.

"Well, I think that is enough for today, you have learnt only the basics that the cross can perform. But they are amongst the most powerful."

He stopped, letting it sink in. Sophia still seemed startled. Barnabe appeared to be in bad need of a drink, his face was pale, the memory of his father's minor ordeal had obviously brought back something more. Maybe it was just Barnabe who feared it, but whatever it was, he now felt that it had resurfaced in his mind.

"Can you find the way back Graciou?"

He nodded and Barnabe left through the passage.

"Are you all right?" Graciou now said to Sophia.

"Yes, I just didn't expect that to happen. It was so bright and he was so fast."

"Neither did I at first, but the shield…"

"I know I've no idea where it came from."

As his gaze began to focus on the background behind, his smile started to fade. In the middle of the silver chamber stood the same man who had beckoned him when he had got Sophia the other day, now it beckoned him once more. How the door to the chamber could even be open he had no idea, but somehow it was.

"Graciou, come on."

Sophia cut through his silent concentration. She was waving him toward her. But his mind still hung on what he had seen.

"What is it?"

Quickly he reacted, looking back toward the chamber once more, only to find the entrance to it closed.

"It's nothing."

Passing back through the translucent wall he stopped for a second, looking back at the passage behind him, before walking back to his fathers quarters.

18

His father's house was warmer than it had been that morning and the fire was now stoked again. They both sat down, as Sophia struck up conversation with him.

"Did Barnabe mention anything about you getting a new cross?"

"Not yet, I'm not sure what will happen."

"I guess they will give you something, it's only a cross after all."

"But it won't be the same if I've not gone through the ceremony." She nodded.

"Well I'm sure they'll sort something out, I never knew they were so powerful."

He smiled.

"Neither did I, till Barnabe showed you."

Sophia sat down next to him. She seemed to be thinking something over.

"Earlier, I heard the soldiers talking about you, they said that the elders wanted you dead. I didn't manage to hear anymore, because they closed the door. But why would they want you dead?"

He thought it over, she continued to stare into his eyes as he looked for an answer.

"Is something wrong?"

He looked up at her, unable to let the question go from his mind. He would have to tell her.

"You know when I told you about the ceremony?"

Her face changed to one of worried confusion.

"Of course, what is it?"

"Well once I had the reaction like you all saw, it seems each of the prophets thought that I wasn't who I was supposed to be. They had decided I wasn't the head of the prophecy."

"But why?" she said half confused.

"Because they thought…"

He stopped, knowing full well she knew nothing of the figures, how would he tell her about this?

"Yes?" she said persistently.

"Whilst I was down in the village, I went into one of the large Manor houses, where I found your mother. She spoke to me for awhile. But when I went back for a second time, someone else was there."

"What do you mean?" she said, sounding intrigued.

"That the prophets thought I was this man, a so called figure, a ghost like creature that haunts whoever it finds, for as long as possible."

Her eyes showed immediate sadness, knowing how her mother had now been treated.

"I didn't want to have to tell you, not like this."

"I had to know sometime."

He got up, walking over to the chair as he put an arm around her.

"That's why they wanted me dead, they thought I wasn't real."

She laughed, half for their stupidity and half for the fact that her mother had not died such a merciful death.

"They said you appeared to know they were coming, I mean they couldn't explain how you managed to deal with their questions so quickly."

He could tell she was veering away from thinking about her mother, but maybe now was not the right time to speak of her.

"Well, after you left the room to tell my father I was awake, I saw something, something entered the room with me. At the foot of my bed."

"What do you mean?"

He had not explained it very well, for he had been the one who had performed the act in the first place.

"Yes, it appeared, but I made it appear. At least I think I did."

"What do you mean you think you made it appear?"

Her face became serious and he became aware that she was becoming impatient.

"I don't know how to tell you, I can't describe what happened, this man wasn't someone I knew."

Her eyes widened, but he could see she had not believed him, for why would she? He struggled in his mind, how could he show her what he had felt and had been feeling?

"Did anyone else see this?"

"No, I was the only one here."

"I'm not sure I believe you Graciou. I mean I believe you say it happened, but it sounds so weird."

He found himself looking around the room, trying to compensate for the fact that he could not show or tell her, what had happened. But as he looked, he found his eyes looking over at the window behind where Sophia was sat, the same question still hanging deep in his thoughts.

As quickly as he had thought it the stained glass began changing colour, mixing in with the white shades that were cast from behind, into the light blue rays now preceding them. A man slowly materialised into view, built from the light that shone through. But unlike the other ghost his eyes were not fixed. They were cast down upon Sophia, pierced by sparkles of tears.

Noticing that he now stood half astounded at the view behind her, she turned to look where Graciou was looking not saying anything for atleast a minute, before one word rang out from her muffled mouth as she spoke.

"Dad?"

Her eyes began to fill and each new tear began to symbolise the grief she had kept for so long. All of her emotions and all of her questions had combined into this moment, for as she stood, she looked upon a face she had not seen for so long. Her hand slid up to the figure's, touching it gently, tears began to fall from it's face, blurring into the grey bristle that patterned the man's old face, mirroring the white of his hair.

"The last time I remember seeing him..."

Sophia stood, shocked and emotional, as she cried not for the loss of her father, but the image of him and his love for her. Walking over to her, Graciou moved a hand out to her, but instead she turned just as he did, placing her head on his shoulder.

"I know, I know."

Holding her gently he felt the sadness she was feeling and knew that the man who had appeared, again by some mysterious form, was certainly Mr Grentshaw.

"I remembered his face as soon as he appeared, he looked the same way he did when I was a little girl."

He smiled down at her, kissing her head softly.

"I guess I better dry these tears, or your father's going to know," she said, worrying unnecessarily.

"It doesn't matter Sophia, he won't care."

She had pulled away from him, drying the tears slowly with the ends of her cardigan and he smiled, unable to see why a girl of such beauty could not be more happy and yet underneath it all, he knew what she was feeling. Behind them both the figure of the man had long since disappeared, but with only his mere presence, it had disturbed a memory for Sophia.

He felt her hand slowly slipping into his, as the culmination of that memory tried to present itself. She nestled her head slowly into his shoulder, as he took her in his arms, caressing her shoulders. Slowly, kissing her once, the same affection returned most intimately without pause and gently they both looked at each other.

As he picked her hand from his, leading her back towards the bed, gently placing her down, her eyes now peaceful and serene as she watched his, deaf only to the sounds of stillness that surrounded them, they gently slipped down between each other. His warmth touched hers as they watched each other, both kissing themselves into rest.

Graciou woke to find her asleep beside him, her eyes still shut gently, and it appeared they had slept undisturbed for quite some time. Lying there he watched her sleeping. The beauty of her face moved him, as he felt her soft breath on the back of his hand. Slowly she began to stir, looking up at him. Smiling silently.

"How long were we asleep?"

"Quite a while."

She propped herself up and he got up off the bed.

"I guess everyone's eating, we can check at least."

She looked over at him as he said it.

"Thank you for showing me that."

He picked her hand up in his.

"You don't have to thank me, if you hadn't have said anything then he would not have appeared."

"I hadn't seen him for so long, so many years."

He smiled as he watched her thinking about it, knowing now that she was at peace over her past and she would no longer carry it around with her.

"Should we walk in together?"

He smiled.

"Come on…"

They both kissed each other once before opening the doorway, as they walked down to the dining area below.

It was still busy outside and many people looked at him as they passed by. Most greeted him, a few stared, but he felt they meant well none-the-less. The eating area was alive with talk and the feeling was much more of rejoicing, as if an old king had returned home to his people. His father cast a gaze over at them as they both walked down the sloping path into the main citadel and they sat down at the table to eat. Many eyes followed them as they did so, but he ignored them as best he could, they were more likely to be staring at him than anything else anyway.

"Good evening, both of you."

Barnabe's voice signalled to them, as they walked up to the table. As well as him and his father, the same men who had brought him in were sat nearby, and the Captain was also sat with them.

"We're glad to here you are on your feet Graciou, wasn't too sure what was happening the other day." said Kurubin over the table.

"Head still hurts a bit, but I woke up feeling all right apart from that."

He caught Sophia's eye again as he stopped speaking.

"I heard that Barnabe was giving you an exercise with the cross earlier."

He looked up at the man who was sat next to him. He was quite skinny and enquired with a sense of intrigue.

"He showed me and Sophia how to open the main door and use the shield."

"Ahh, did it go well?"

"Sophia amazed us earlier, the shield she made was nearly the same strength as Excem's." Barnabe had spoken from further down the table and the man turned to look in his direction.

His father looked up then, over at Sophia smiling.

"Well it's nice to know someone else has a hidden power too."

Everyone smiled as he said it, a few stopped eating.

"Was it your sword you used?" Kurubin said.

"There were pieces of it everywhere," Barnabe said, pausing before carrying on. "Lost most of it. It was magnificent though, amazing for someone who's never even touched a cross before."

Both Barnabe and his father exchanged subtle glances over the food and he continued to eat. His father had said hello the same as Barnabe as they had entered, but was proving rather quiet as the night progressed.

Continuing to try and catch his eye as the meal proceeded to be consumed, he failed to do so. Gradually the meal was eaten, each of them full, they began to relax in their chairs.

Most of the men had walked away from the table saying their goodbyes for the evening. Only Sophia, Barnabe, his father and himself remained.

"Well, I think I shall bid you good evening. I wish you all a good night's rest."

Barnabe got up from the table and both Sophia and himself said good-night to him. His father was still quiet and had not said anything for a long time. Unable to bear the silence any longer he spoke.

"Father are you..."

His face looked drawn and saddened.

"It's nothing. I think I will be going as well, goodnight to the both of you."

Excem smiled at Sophia and softly patted her on the shoulder as he left.

"I don't know why my father is so quiet," he said later to Sophia as they left the eating area.

"Maybe he's just remembering something," she said.

"I have no idea what it might be though."

"Well ask him when you go in, I'm sure he's not going to bite your head off."

He smiled and took his hand out of hers, as it had been since they had walked up from the eating area. Kissing her gently on the lips he bid her good night and walked up to his house. Opening the doorway he found his father by the fire, with a glass of something a lot stronger than tea or water in his hand.

"I know something's wrong."

His father carried on staring into the crackling fire, which had been re-lit since he left. Then his father turned, his face looking haunted.

"You know, I remember," his eyes were welling, each of them breaking with tears beginning to fall quickly to his lap, "I remember her face..."

He thought for a second, but it didn't take him too long to guess.

"My mother?"

"I have one image of her, one image stowed away in my mind, the only one."

He continued to watch as his father spoke, feeling the sadness from him.

"I saw you both earlier."

Graciou looked up, unsure of where he might have seen them, before or after they had come into the dining area.

"You did?"

"Yes and it reminded me of her, seeing the both of you there, remind-ed me of how it was when she was still with us."

Graciou smiled, trying his best to comfort his father.

"I can barely remember it..."

He knew it was a pathetic reply, but he knew not what else to say.

"You were very young, I don't expect you to remember it all."

His father's eyes were heavy, with a sadness he had only seen once before, when Harrass had died. Now his mind was cast back to when he was only a few years old and yet he remembered it vividly. He repeated the image in his mind, wondering what truly had happened that day, but still unprepared to ask his father about it.

"There was something else there that day."

He said, sure now of it's origin, his father looking up at him.

"The storm had begun to form across the horizon, I had been watching it and saw the rock fall down toward me."

He continued.

"It was like the Acias..."

His father's head began to shake from side to side.

"It couldn't have been the Acias, the Grentshaws always kept it in the same place. Besides that, it has never harmed any person who was friend to it, only foe."

"Then what was it?"

"After she fell everything became a blur, but I remember seeing the sky just as you did."

"But that day the Storm hit, that morning I was in school, I saw the same thing."

His father straightened in his chair.

"What do you mean?"

"I saw a rock fall from the sky, I was transfixed on the clouds, if it hadn't have been for the teacher..."

He trailed off, unable to think of his life ending so short.

"What?"

"When she took me back upstairs after it had passed, a huge rock lay where I had been sat."

He saw his father's face turn white as he said it.

"But Marcus told me that there hadn't been any damage to that room."

Astounded he continued.

"Marcus..." he said, in slight shock.

"Yes?" his father said bemused.

"I still find it strange that Marcus was host to such a creature, he seemed so composed."

His father looked over at him.

"Maybe he was composed, I've never seen someone cope with a host inside them, it's something that truly ravages a person, but if he survived for that long...He must have been stronger than all of us put together."

Graciou nodded.

"That day when we left the dunes, I think he may have thought to sacrifice himself to save us, he was so adamant that we get free of the Storm."

"But he still appeared at your house near the woods as well?"

Graciou wondered why it might have been.

"He did yes, maybe I'll never know why, but from the way he acted it was in his own way I guess, a way for him to guard me against what was within him. He could not stop the figure, and it did not pass onto me after it left."

"Was there anyone else in the room with you?"

"Just me at the time, Mary came in later."

"Then it's likely it scattered from the building, maybe even died where it stood. Who knows though truly?"

Graciou kept his eyes fixed on his father, sure of his words and yet he felt his father knew how sure he was of them too.

His father stood up, looking serious.

"It may explain why we were so easily and so quickly taken over by the Storm, I never suspected him of being subject to a figure, but it seems he may have been for a long time. That kind of strain can do awful things to a person."

Graciou for a moment thought he might understand some of what it was these figures produced to gain such control over there host.

"I fear the figures may have something of a dual purpose."

"What are you saying?" Graciou replied, unsure of his notion.

"I'm saying that the figures conjure images, images that can be believable and images that cannot be broken without great will of mind. If they indeed had taken Marcus over, they could have created anything in place of death, in place of suffering or merely in place of his ability to tell life from death."

"You mean to say that no matter what they put him through there was a reason for his final journey?"

"I'm sure there was a reason for all of it Graciou, the power they wield is immense, not even I can stop them from conjuring the images they produce."

Graciou felt as if his father spoke from a different place now, it was an open place, defenceless, fearful and yet angry to fight, where memories collided with each other, to form a subdued sense of regret.

"Do not worry about them Graciou, they cannot hurt us here. The crosses protect us from whatever they might try to do."

He smiled. His father's strength at least was still intact.

"Get some rest Graciou, you can sleep in the bed tonight."

He got up and went to make the bed for the night, turning back to his father for a second.

"Are you sure you'll be all right?"

His father turned back, with a smile on his face.

"Don't worry about me, you just get some rest."

For the first few hours, Graciou tried frantically to get to sleep, his mind filled with the memories that the conversation with his father had stirred. But eventually as weariness took him, he fell asleep.

His eyes flew open. Only a few hours had passed and yet the room was pitch black. He had a sickening feeling in his stomach, as if his insides were freezing over, and the very thought made him feel worse. The sheets on his bed he had thrown around and he knew he had been dreaming nightmares, but had no recollection of them. His father was asleep in the chair and his drink had spilt out over the floor, at least what had been left of it.

Clothed and weary he left the room, hoping that the cooler air outside might make him feel somewhat better. But he felt no change as he left the room, the coldness of the marble floors stabbing at his feet. Dropping down onto his knees he grabbed his stomach, the excruciating pain was overwhelming.

With no idea of what it was, he got up and started to walk towards the medical ward. The nurse surely would be awake, or at least half awake. As he climbed over the last step and looked down toward her door, all he could see was darkness, like a shroud about him. Deciding it would be best he got back to his room he turned for a second, seeing the translucent doorway off to the side of him.

Stopping he turned. Something dark shimmered and whirled behind the doorway. He hoped desperately that whatever he had just seen was not there, unsure whether this was part of some lurid nightmare he could not wake from. But again he saw it. Another set of shadows walked past the doorway this time in the direction of the hearth at the far end, each appearing to know where it was going.

Walking forward, he tried to keep a steady footing. His mind somehow numbed the pain that was in his abdomen, which was now blinding all but his senses. The figures had stopped moving out of sight. But even when he thought they might have turned and fled, or somehow dissapeared, once more another moved across it yet again, it's form smooth and effortless.

Slowly, it sunk it's body into the cold wall beginning to move toward him. Faintly he could hear footsteps and a clattering of feet behind him. The figure bore through the last of the doorway and was surveying him. It's eyes were grey and stark in difference to his own. He surveyed the creature back, without fear and without emotion. His entire body had become numb, his eyes unwavering, behind him voices were shouting at him, one of which he identified as his father.

"Graciou!"

"Get away from it!"

But he was unable to move. It's eyes continued to match his, and then with a quick jerk he felt his eyes pulling away, his father striding out in front of him, cross bared. Falling back he watched his father's hand move forward, as the creature itself was pushed further and further back through the doorway, it's eyes fixed upon his father's face.

"GET BACK!" his father roared in it's direction.

As it began to slowly back down, something inside it had given way and as it fled they followed it, out of his and everyone else's view. His father instantly turned to his side.

"My God, are you all right?"

"I couldn't move," he said, shivering wildly in his father's arms. His sense of feeling had come back, but how the pain had come and gone so quickly, he did not know.

"What the hell was it?"

"I don't know, I've never seen it before."

The other men looked worried by what he had said. From the left side Barnabe came running up the stairs.

"You four, get some weapons and guard that doorway with your life. If the slightest flicker occurs across that wall, shoot the hell out of it."

Barnabe was ferocious, his mind sinking into the objective, as was the way of his tactically minded brain.

"What happened Excem?"

The Storms of Acias

His father looked up at Barnabe.

"I came running out to find him here, half dressed, transfixed by whatever that is."

"What did it look like?" Barnabe said to him.

"I've never seen it before Barnabe."

His voice sounded slightly erratic, scared that all their preparations here and elsewhere might be in jeopardy.

"We need to get Graciou down to the barracks."

His father nodded, but Graciou stopped him.

"No, I must stay here, that thing didn't look at me for no reason. I'm not going anywhere until it's left here altogether."

Barnabe thought for a second about arguing the point.

"All right, but if you stay here, stay out of the way of things."

He gave him a pat on the back. Graciou looked round, feeling completely useless. Quickly he picked up a gun from the wall, forming up with the others his rifle pointed in the direction of the doorway. The man from the other evening was next to him.

"What did it look like Graciou? Barnabe ran us out of our houses and our beds faster than I've ever seen before."

"Just keep a steady aim, whatever it is, we're not letting it get in here."

The man aimed his gun at the gap where the translucent wall had fallen away, the same place where the entity had appeared, whatever it had been. Both his father and Barnabe had walked off somewhere else in the citadel, he guessed to tell the others of what was happening and make adequate preparations.

However hard his mind tried, he was still unable to cast the figure's eyes from his, and they haunted his gaze even now. His body was now feverish and the sweat had begun to drip from his forehead. With all the commotion inside the castle and the numbing he had felt when it had stared at him, he hadn't noticed the pain slowly creeping back in on him. But whatever it was he wasn't going to let it take him over. Above all else he was going to stay side by side with these men and make sure they were safe.

The seconds slowly turned over in his mind, setting themselves into minutes and then hours, without a sign of anything in front of them. His arm had gone lazy and his head was now beating harder and faster than he had ever felt anything before, his body was overridden by something, something he had no name for.

"God, you're sweating like crazy, are you all right?"

He tried not to answer, but he knew he'd only get asked again.

"Ever since I woke, I've been feeling strange, I have no idea what it is."

"You should…"

His voice stopped, a white shimmer had glided across the wall, various guns became rigid beside him, as he himself straightened his own gun, each one following the white glimmer as it vanished into the wall and then started back across it again.

"Sir? Sir?!" One of the other men shouted close to him.

"I'm here…" Barnabe said, appearing somewhere behind them.

"Move back from the wall, quickly!"

Each of them slowly moved back.

"They might be trying to get in, whoever the hell they are."

"I thought we knew," one of them said.

"Even if it is them, how did they get past our sentries?"

They had backed off and now there was at least ten feet between them and the wall. Each of them still had their guns held high. But his head was starting to vibrate. The force inside his skull was immense, like it was crushing him from the outside in.

"Graciou?"

He turned his head toward him, trying desperately to make it look as if he was all right. But it was no use and with a massive cry he dropped his gun, clasping his head tightly, trying to stop it from shaking.

"Graciou?! What's wrong?"

All he could manage was to stare up at Barnabe as he kneeled in front of him.

"GRACIOU?!"

Behind them the wall had started to vibrate. Turning on his knees, he faced it, moving toward it slowly. His eyes and head, as well as his throat, were tightly contorted. How he was breathing he knew not, and how he was thinking, he had no idea at all.

As he drew closer the shaking intensified and he felt as if every blood vessel inside his veins were trapped. Until finally, he reached the wall, stretching out a hand to the now cracked face. Behind him Barnabe was shouting him down, but had not yet resorted to grabbing him and the men had let their weapons drop. His mouth let out a few words as he pushed his hand against the cool marble surface.

"Keep away!"

The Storms of Acias

The words had come out and he knew not where they had come from. Each word rang out around him and as he drove his hand on to the cold marble surface, the doorway opened once more, his hand and head falling through onto the cold stone floor below. Gunfire issued from behind him, but it appeared only one or two people were firing. His head slowly began to soften, his body began to calm itself, each of his legs and arms started to stop shaking. His head stopped its merciless shaking as the last of the gunfire faded from his ears, blacking out everything.

19

He woke gently, still able to feel the tiredness in his body.

"How are you feeling?"

The voice sounded familiar, it was Sophia beside him again.

"Somewhat better."

"Seems you're in this bed quite a lot," she laughed. He choked as he tried to laugh too.

"Would appear so…" he replied.

"Everyone's talking about you again, most of the soldiers see you as some kind of saint. Your father had to stop them from coming in and pledging allegiance to you."

His head just felt worse at that prospect, yet he understood why they might feel that way. Lifting his hand out from the sheets he held hers tightly.

"I blacked out, what happened?"

Another voice was nearby. It was the Captain this time.

"You were crawling toward the door when I saw you, I had my gun ready. I don't really know why, but I knew something was going to happen. Once the door opened, well let's just say they weren't ready for us."

"Do we know who they are now?"

"Seems they are part of the same people who attacked us all those years ago. We can't be completely certain, but they wear the same clothes, carry the same weaponry. They even tried to fight the same way."

He remembered his father's words and knew fairly instantly that it must have been some sort of trickery and yet, it could have been as real as it looked. The thought scared him through and through. His father was sat down in the chair by the fire and was already faced in his direction.

"Glad you're feeling better."

His body felt so weak.

"I don't understand what happened to me."

"We best keep that between us, I'm afraid it's not only the men who are talking."

He turned toward the Captain, still having his eyes half on his father.

"Oh don't worry, Kurubin knows what's going on, but it might be best if not everyone knows yet."

"Well, whatever it is they think, I don't very much care."

His head was weary once more and he placed it back down onto the cushion, falling back to sleep.

She was still there when he woke, his eyes were open for a change and though he felt groggy, he was able to get up.

"How long have you been sat there?"

"Quite a while, since yesterday at least. I slept while you did."

"You didn't have to do that," he said to her, knowing that she was waiting here on him a lot now.

"I wanted to Graciou. Besides your father let me in and sat me down after I'd asked about you, I had no choice," she smiled.

He got up, dressing himself slowly, wondering what might be happening outside.

"So what's it like out there now?"

"Well they've placed at least eight men at the main doorway, they don't appear to be going anywhere."

"But I thought they managed to kill those that entered."

She stood up and walked over to him.

"I was of that opinion as well and from what I can gather they did."

"Well, I doubt they'll stop me from going up there."

They both walked out from the room and onto the marble steps.

"You want to go up there?" She asked, now seeing the defiance in his voice.

"It's all right, I feel a lot better now I'm still interested to see what's happening. Something really strange happened up there."

There were quite a few men at the top of the stairwell and Kurubin was one of them. As they began to walk up he placed his gun down and walked over to them.

"I'm glad you're feeling better, but I wouldn't advise being outside right now."

He appeared hurried, as if he didn't want him to see something, or he didn't want someone to see him.

"Make what they will of it Kurubin, but I'm not staying in that room forever."

He was a little surprised by the way he forced it, but since the other day he had changed, he felt as if his mind were building strength within him. Most of the men were quite pleased to see him and several turned round to greet him.

"How are you feeling sir?"

"Much better thank you, I take it none of you were hurt the other day?"

"No, most of us were fine, the group you're talking about are mostly downstairs, apart from the odd few. It's nice to see you up and about sir."

He smiled, turning back to Kurubin, walking over to him so he could whisper.

"How come we haven't moved back into the chambers yet?"

Kurubin paused, collecting his thoughts, then spoke.

"Well, when I started firing into that gap the other day, I counted at least a dozen of them. Once the rest of the men had got clean shots and started to fire, it was more like three or four left. We moved in further yesterday and found four of them hiding in the silver chamber, but there's one missing. None of us can find him, we've looked and looked." Kurubin was puzzled.

"And you're sure he's not a figure right?"

"He's definitely not that. But what makes it really strange is that he was the one standing over you on the other side of the door, when you collapsed. He had both of his hands pressed against the marble, his face was strange, and cold like ice."

"What's been decided by my Father about it all?"

"He's been talking with the Elders since this morning but I've not got anything yet."

He bid him goodbye for now and walked back into his father's house, Sophia still with him. He wished he could go and find that thing, wherever it hid, as if somehow he knew a better way, but the inability to know where it was frustrated him.

Sophia sat down, looking as calm as ever.

"What are you thinking about?"

"I just wish we knew where that thing was. I should have…"

He was unsure what he should have done exactly, but he should have done something, he was sure of that.

"You couldn't have done anything more Graciou, you might be experiencing some pretty strange stuff lately, but what could you have done?"

"I'm not sure, I just don't like thinking of it, out there waiting."

She stopped and he could tell she was a little disgruntled, only slightly, but still he could feel it. As if he should have listened to what she had to say more.

His father came in minutes later, looking annoyed.

"What did they say?"

Sophia had thought ahead of him and he could hear the apprehension in her voice.

"They're sending Barnabe back in there soon. They said you should stay here. The Elders overheard you were out there earlier and nearly went crazy. They're getting really quite controlling about this whole thing."

He wanted desperately to go and assist Barnabe, but he knew that his father would not allow it, even though on another note Graciou knew he would want to.

"So I have to remain confined here now?"

"Well I won't stop you leaving if you really want to, but it's probably best. They're getting very agitated."

"Why are they being like this? It doesn't make any sense."

His father smiled.

"Some people aren't quite as singular in their objectives as we are. They've been following in the paths of your prophecy for over five hundred years. Their view of power and how they wield it has become very distorted in places."

He smiled again as he finished the sentence, but it was a smile of sadness. He knew his father had hoped for better than this. But slowly he had stopped pushing for it.

They waited again for what felt like quite a few hours, before Barnabe stepped into the doorway. He stood there, looking anxious.

"I've been sent here to get you Graciou."

His father turned in the chair.

"Who by?"

"I found it Excem."

His father's eyes rose.

"Where?"

"It showed itself freely, I have four men waiting with it right now, I must hurry Excem. It has asked to see Graciou, he identified him by name."

"Hang on Barnabe, I don't want him near that thing yet."

"Excem I don't want those men put in jeopardy, we have no idea what it might do."

Graciou interjected, knowing what he had to do.

"I'll go speak with it, and whatever it wants to know, or say, I'll deal with it."

His father paused, turning back to him, "I can't stop you, but watch him, never turn your back on him."

He smiled at Sophia as he left, following Barnabe out of the door.

The path that Barnabe took was flanked by people, men who uttered no words as he passed them. The arrival hall was dark and cold as he entered it. Inside his body he began to feel the intense pain once more, but he beat it down inside him, not letting it take over his mental focus. Barnabe entered into the room, stopping as he turned back to face the door

"Are you sure you're ready Graciou?"

He nodded, not wanting to back down at this point. Already he had spotted a group of men, each with a rifle pointed in it's direction, each looking fixed to the target, unwavering. The creature, whatever it was, could see him coming. One of it's dark grey eyes flicked across in his direction, then back to a distant spot it had been focusing on. It surveyed him as he walked out in front of it, taking it's time before it spoke.

"Who are you?" it's cold voice asked.

"I am Graciou Excemaratis."

It surveyed him again, it's voice rough like badly carved stone.

"Why are you so powerful?"

It's question was one he had not thought it would ask, and he felt the men around him flinch, but he knew not why.

"Am I so powerful?"

Its eyes widened.

"I have seen your power crush mine without remorse."

"Are you speaking of when I fell to the floor?"

It nodded with great stiffness in it's body, as if it were coiled like a spring for attack.

"Why are you here? You have no business with my people," he had said it without even thinking of the words.

"No, I am here because I was sent here. Before I depart, I must ask one more thing."

Behind him weapons were raised and he signalled for them to be lowered.

"Speak of it."

"Why were you so sad at your mother's death?"

The question hit him like a piercing sword, slicing into him like an old wound being torn open from long ago. The memory had lain still and silent within him, but now it shot to the forefront of his mind and a tremendous rage built within him. Composing himself he tried to stay controlled and firm.

"I was not sad, at the time I felt no emotion."

"No, but now I feel it."

"I would urge you not to enquire upon these lines."

"I have seen what I speak of, so where is the harm in bringing it up?"

Without a second pause he lunged forward, grabbing it's throat in one swoop of his hand, overpowering the object that was now firmly placed against the wall.

"Did you stand there whilst she fell, did you laugh as she tumbled to her own death?" Graciou's grip tightening around it.

His voice had become empowered and Barnabe had not told the men to fire or move forward, though he could feel the anger rising inside of him too.

"I may not speak of such things, I come only as a messenger."

"Then why did you try to attack us?"

It's eyes narrowed onto his.

"My men were my shield, to use them to get to you, to deliver a message I knew I had to."

"What message!"

His anger was taking over and he thrust it harder against the wall.

"That you must be watchful of the one that at first, you cannot see, the one who is covered in shadow. For he will try to lead you astray."

"You've tried to lead my people astray before now, why should I trust your word?"

"Because I have come here alone and without the shackles of my master. I have come here to give you this message."

He gave the creature a long and hard look. He believed what it was he had to say, but was not prepared to start trusting it.

"Stay here, I need to speak about this."

It nodded, meekly.

Barnabe was stood just behind him, overseeing them all and as he turned, the others replaced their rifles onto their target.

"What did it say?"

"It's a trick, it cannot be anything else. It's words are incoherent and of no interest, insistent…"

His voice broke off, as behind a few haphazard shots were fired, one ricocheting off the wall near to them. Barnabe instantly threw an arm over his shoulder and dropped to the ground.

"STOP CREATURE!" Barnabe roared at it.

The creature wa. running towards the men. Most had tried to defend themselves, but the accuracy of their shots was poor. Thankfully, as the beast tried to run across the chamber to the far doorway, one of the men managed to place a hit, instantly knocking him down.

"Good shooting men!" Barnabe shouted as he got to his feet Graciou got up to head for the creature.

"I knew you were not to be trusted," Graciou shouted over at it, just able to hear it's last few words.

"The shadowed man will come in trust, but do not be fooled by his appearance, for he is not as he appears."

Graciou disgusted, turned to Barnabe, making it clear what should take place.

"I'll deal with this, get back to your father and tell him what's happened."

No sooner had he got to the doorway than his father was already asking him what had happened and why he looked so flustered.

"I'm all right."

"What happened?" Sophia said instantly, mimicking his father.

"It was another figure," he said, sitting down slowly in the chair that his father had got up from.

"But I thought?"

"So did Barnabe. I turned my back on it once, Barnabe made sure he watched it. But it ran for each of the men not much later."

"Were they hurt?" Sophia said anxiously.

"No, it's not them."

"Then what's bothering you? What did it say?"

He would have thought it was obvious, had it not been for the fact that the figure's words, though he was sure were not to be trusted, somehow laid a path of doubt in his mind.

"It spoke about a man I could not see, someone who would try to lead me astray." Graciou shook his head.

"But I doubt now that it has any validity."

His father looked to be deep in thought as he had said it.

"I think we need to speak with the highest of the prophets, alone and without counsel. I think it is about time we asked him a few questions and he might be able to shed light on who or whatever this person is."

"But surely…"

"Graciou, that thing did not come here to show us mercy or give us information. It came here to hurt as many people as it could, and in the process, it may well have slipped out information about something it should not have done."

His father stepped toward the doorway, opening it, looking back for a minute.

"I shall go and speak with him first. Wait here, I will come back once he is ready to talk with us."

His father left and he sat back down with Sophia, who now looked a little confused.

"What happened outside didn't sound that nice," she said.

"Do you remember a man called Marcus?"

She looked enquiringly at him.

"No, who was he?"

"He was a Captain like Kurubin, who got separated from my father and yourself when you came here."

"What of him Graciou?"

"He came to me while I was with Mary, past the Acias. He came to me in a state of disillusion, talking about all the wrongs he had done and sounding much like he was some sort of mad man. As soon as the room was lit I found a mangled figure before me, it had stopped resembling him quite some time ago, but none the less it was Marcus."

"That sounds pretty horrible, but what's that got to do with what happened just now?"

"The man who asked to speak to me had the same sort of look about him, his eyes wandered the same as Marcus's had. He spoke with the same sort of scared voice, as if he were being watched."

"What are you getting at Graciou?"

"That something might have sent him here, to tell me something important and that my father, who is so quick to look at only what he sees, as Barnabe is also, will not see what he cannot see."

She looked now more confused than before, but also as if he were mad.

"I see nothing more Graciou. I think your father is right to speak to the prophets, they hold as much knowledge as anyone here. Maybe they will know more of it."

"Maybe," he said, still thinking upon it.

Their conversation soon ended and they were each left to their thoughts, as the minutes steadily rolled by.

The door opened and his father strode in, with a look of satisfaction on his face.

"They've agreed to speak with you, as long as I'm there."

"Did they protest much?" he said as he got up.

"Yes, but I managed to make them listen to me."

"When did they say we could go?" Graciou looked up at him.

"They say they're busy, but I think they will want to get this over with."

"Let's go then."

Both of them left the house, walking up the stone steps that he had used to get to the ceremony room earlier. It was lit the same, as it had been the last time he had been there, and there was a doorway at the far side, which he had not noticed before.

They both walked into the room. He could see a set of rows at the back of the room. Each row had cushioned blood red benches, stretching up toward the ceiling. At the front there was a lectern, where a round staircase descended down underneath it. His father led him through it and they both walked into yet another room.

"This is the main meeting room for the prophets and ourselves, he said we should wait here."

Sitting down, they each waited patiently, as the prophet walked in not much later. His clothes were red, the same as the seats. The prophet's face was bony and his skin pale. His hair had once been dark brown but was now grey. Barely looking at either of them, he stood at the lectern, as if he were about to preach.

"Good evening to you. I hear that you wish to speak with me Graciou?"

His father signalled to him to speak.

"Yes, earlier the creature that was outside," he seemed to cringe as he said it. "Told me that I had to be wary of some man, someone that I could not see, what do you think he might have meant?"

Graciou watched as the prophet's eyes narrowed. His father watched intently, wondering what had been so important.

"I know of no such form, only that of the great dark."

Graciou's mind lit up, seeing that he was letting some of what he knew through.

"What of the great dark?"

The prophet for a minute did not answer, but then he saw that he had no choice.

"Your council with that creature disturbs me."

"How so?"

"I am afraid to talk of what it has said, for those words may be a trap for us all."

He looked at his father. The lunacy of this man was too much to bear, he did not even presume to hear him through.

"You have no need to worry, his words were only heard by myself."

"It is not the bearer I worry for, but the words themselves."

His father interjected.

"Cut your rambling augury and answer my son's questions."

He waited and then asked again.

"So what is this great dark?"

"Seeing as I have no choice in the matter, I must speak candidly. The 'Great dark' is a very old term, we use it to brand the storm's occurrence, but they seem to call it the 'Great shadow'."

His father looked confused and slightly astounded.

"You know who they are?"

"Yes Excemaratis, they came before us, they believe that we are a scourge upon their ground. Since the first day of the prophecy being given to us we were to expect something all-together different than we have got."

Stopping his father's anger from over spilling, Graciou answered back.

"Then what is it that the prophecy told you to expect augury?"

"Many things and nothing at all. The prophecy speaks in riddles and is largely inconsistent, we have on many occasions tried to decode it and for the larger part we have only been able to manage that 'A young boy would come, who is the keeper of the word.' That word of course being Gracious, as the prophecy dictates. It also dictated that you would be called Graciou by birth."

"Word being Gracious?" Graciou asked, wondering what the prophet meant.

"The prophecy also stated that you would carry the word of Gracious, we still aren't sure what that means. But most always thought it meant you would speak the language of Gracious."

He wondered what that could mean, because he had never heard of any language that went by that name, and why he would suddenly come to speak it, was hard to understand.

"Surely you must know what the rest of it translates into?" his father said.

"Only the parts I have just dictated, the rest of it speaks of several things, none of which make sense."

"Well if it doesn't make sense, how can we call it a prophecy?" he said.

"Because of who delivered it," the augury paused and then continued. "He was a very old man, older than any of us here. He came to your forth great grandfather while he was out walking amongst the plains, foretelling of a boy who would come and be named Graciou, also stating the word of Gracious and Graciou would hold great importance for all."

He stopped, beginning to reduce his talking to a whisper.

"When asked why my ancestor should even believe what he was saying, he gave him something. To this day we still have replicas of the first, that of the cross we each wear." Returning to his normal tone, he finished. "Make of that what you will, we will believe it to be that he was the first of the prophets, sent to us from a divine presence. It is in him we have lain our faith for so long."

"Thank you for your time augury," his father said, returning to look at Graciou.

The prophet nodded and they got up from the seat they had both taken.

As they were walking out, questions of the prophet's words came flooding into his mind.

"Did you know he knew any of this?"

"I never had thought to ask. The prophets have never lied, but then again they have always hidden some truth. Let us hope we know of the finer integrity of all that truth for now. Whoever this man was, he knew a lot about you, but how he works into it all I have no idea."

He continued to think about what his father said, as they both walked back down to their house. Why had his father not known of this a very long time ago? What was so important that it had to be kept so far from his father's own mind? None of it made sense.

20

The days rolled into one another and he continued to talk with Sophia and the rest of his family. But none of the conversations bore any new insight. Each of them was dumb-founded by what the prophet had said. Still none of them knew who the man was that had appeared, but why would they? For he would have come so many generations before them, it was as if they had uncovered a lie that everyone seemed bent on unravelling, but they could not.

Walking into the house he sat himself down into one of the chairs, the fire roaring in front of him. For a second he thought something moved out of the far corner of his eye. But he instantly forgot it, putting it down to a trickery of the flames flickering against the hearth. Again he saw the strange movement and unsure of what he had seen, looked around for its origin. For a moment he couldn't believe what he was seeing, in the other chair sat a gaunt and unrecognisable face.

"Who's there?"

It paused and he moved trying to get a better look at it.

"It's been along time Graciou."

It's speech was contorted with the inability to speak whole words.

"Who are you?"

For some reason his mind did not tell him to stand, nor get a better view of the man who he spoke to. His mind was strangely at peace.

"My name is unimportant," it continued. "I have come to deliver a message, one that only you can hold, one that only you need to know of."

It paused again.

"Your each and every step is watched by a person you cannot see, nor hear. I must urge you to watch over yourself in the next few days, for…"

He was cut short, as the doorway flew open behind him and he stood up, his eyes fixed upon the prophet who now stood there.

"Prophet?" he said, astonished.

But instead of speech, he began to hear a noise, which started to fill his ears, deeper and more powerful than anything he had ever heard before. Filling his mind with a blank confusion, stopping his thoughts and balance in motion. Falling to the ground he watched the counsellor, his eyes staring blankly toward the far wall.

Desperately he tried to speak, but already the sound was too much for him to bear and he could feel every inch of the room vibrating. For a moment, he thought it was himself again, but he felt nothing within himself, then realised that the prophet must be the one causing it. Wood began to snap and splinter under the vibrations around the walls, other noises and crashes intermingled with that of the sound he could hear. The fire roaring behind him, flames licking every part of the fireplace. The prophet fell to the ground, the person he had been speaking to seconds earlier not now the person who was slumped against the floor.

"Prophet?! Are you all right?"

Outstretching his hand he helped him to turn over, his eyes were dazzled and each looked completely without sight.

"Something's wrong Graciou, something...ahh..."

His screaming was persistent at whatever pain continued to consume him.

"You must find your father quickly, you must be safe!"

And as he said those last few words, he felt the citadel itself starting to crumble and fall. Outside the doorway each of the walls and floor vibrated so heavily that he was finding it hard to stand up. His father was at the door, his hand on his shoulders, quickly and persistently leading him from the room.

"Wait...What about Sophia and the others?"

"I shall go and find her, get outside of the citadel Graciou!"

For a second he watched him dart away, as dust and small chunks of rock began to fall from the ceiling above him. But realising the great danger that was now looming above, he ran in the opposite direction, continuing to the Arrival Hall, where he waited for the others.

The chambers were filling slowly with people, but the numbers were decreasing as he watched, with fewer and fewer coming out. He wondered if he should dart in too. But seconds later his father appeared, with Sophia beside him. He swiftly supported her. She had been cut in quite a few different places and looked out of breath.

"Are you all right?"

"Yes, I'll be all right."

Quickening their pace they darted out into the silver chamber, where Barnabe was already waiting.

"Where are the other men Barnabe?"

"I sent them in to find the others, do you have any idea what's happening?"

His father looked around at him, as if he knew. But he remained silent, for even though there had indeed been strange events just now, he did not deem it important to tell either of them at this moment.

"We've no idea, but the citadel's falling to pieces..."

The entrance to the citadel was deluged in rubble and dust. For a moment Graciou could not believe what was truly taking place. He was just able to see Kurubin and a few other men and women walking free of the entrance as the dust started to fill the air. Most people around him rushed over, as did he Barnabe started to move the others into the golden chamber.

His father put an arm under Kurubin, who seemed to have somehow hurt his leg.

"Let's get into the other chamber," his father shouted quickly, helping Kurubin as best he could, as one of the other men assisted his father.

Slowly the rumbling had begun to lessen and there was no sign of more rubble or debris falling. He stared into the open gap just above the top of the rocks, now wondering what the hell had just happened.

They each huddled together at the far side of the wall. Some already knew that the structure had collapsed completely, some of the women and children still stood as if more were to come. But as he looked back, he knew the worst, which was that they would not be coming out anytime soon.

"Barnabe."

Barnabe turned round to meet his father, as his concentrated face changed to that of disbelief.

"How many did you send in?" his father said, slowly and with shocked disbelief.

"A dozen..." Barnabe said, unable to believe that only four remained.

"How many were inside?"

"Too many Excem...too many."

His father walked over to him.

"What happened Graciou? Are you hurt?"

Knowing he had no choice but to answer, he replied slowly and cautiously.

"No I'm fine, just a few cuts and bruises."

"What happened in there?"

Graciou replied slowly, trying to remember it all in a coherent manner.

"He stormed into the room, that's when the noise started outside I didn't know what was going on…"

Still in shock he held Sophia closer to him, both of them half shaking from what had happened, clothes caked in dust from the debris.

"The prophet?"

"Yes, I can't figure…" Graciou looked back, at a loss for words.

"Try and see if you can help them, see if they need you."

He gave them both a smile and they both walked off into the crowd, looking for people who might need their help.

His father, Barnabe and Kurubin all walked over to the doorway and began talking fervently, raising their voices every few moments. But all he could think about in the back of his mind was of the man and what he said, and why it was the prophet had come into the room. It was as if he had been trying to protect him from another force completely, maybe that of the force he had been speaking to? But the man didn't feel like someone he couldn't trust. In fact he felt as if he were trying to protect him, but so was the prophet it seemed. No explanation he could think of fitted or made sense.

His father walked over at that moment.

"Did you get out in one piece?" he looked up quickly.

"Yes, I managed."

Graciou stared at his father, able to feel the grief in not just his father's heart, but also that of everyone around him.

"Well, we have decided to depart from here in the morning, that's a few hours from now, you should both get some rest."

He nodded back at him and his father walked away.

It was now obvious that the people who had been trapped inside weren't about to be rescued, and for that he and everyone else around him grieved. Both of them rested together at the side of one of the great walls. The chamber wasn't heated and he found it hard to get to sleep, but eventually he did. For most of the early morning he continued to stay awake, as did plenty of other people around him. Women were crying in pockets and men silently grieved, some comforted by friends, others by complete strangers, but he felt their grief more than anything as he lay there.

The others he watched, sleeping in uncomfortable and confused dreams no doubt. Some of the soldiers were as unable to sleep as him. He was just able to hear them talking. A small dimly lit light cascaded out from where their voices issued, setting a deep glow into the chamber walls around.

"Doesn't make any sense, why did the place just start falling to pieces?"

"If you ask me it was something to do with Graciou, I went past his place and one of the Prophets was lying dead."

"Dead?" the man seemed to say incredulously

"That's right, just lying there, not moving or anything."

"Could you see how he might have died?" the other man had said.

"Not sure, I don't think Graciou did it, but it just didn't look right."

He heard a hush come from the other side and suddenly the chatter stopped, light slowly shutting off, the warming glow quickly receding into the darkness. Next to him Sophia was shivering, he placed an arm around her as he looked back out across the rest of the chamber, wondering what the new day would bring.

His dreams were filled with an incoherent smothering of pictures, all squashed together and out of shape. He tried but could not sort them in his head. He managed to catch a glimpse of one. It was of a man stood up, looking around, his eyes casting over every object he saw around him, trying to find something of familiarity. He hadn't noticed as he had been watching, but now his eyes were on Graciou and he appeared to start shouting, his words trapped within the squashed frame, as it tried to dash out of view. But he caught it, just as a few words came through.

"Watch the storm, now more than ever it will try to hurt that which you love most."

The picture quickly darted from view, leaving him to the squashed images, all jostling for position within his head. As his mind began to turn, thinking of what had happened, he woke.

The room was still dark. No one spoke or stirred around him. The crying had stopped now, but that wasn't to say people weren't still there, now they just sat in silence, with spent tears that would never be able to bring back the dead. His dream came back to him with a sudden shock and he tried to remember all of what had been said. Who was this man? Why did he keep following him? Unable now to sleep and unable for sure to suppress his thoughts to give him that sleep, he lay awake, watching the chamber ceiling around him.

As early morning began to rise outside, the faintest of blue light cascaded over each of the golden walls, slowly beginning to glisten with a golden hue. Around him people had started to stir, looking weary-eyed and some remembering the previous day sooner than they had hoped. He, however had not slept at all, unable to stop thinking of what had happened. Sophia woke beside him and lifted her head up from where it was now resting, on his chest.

"Looks like we're getting ready to go," she said to him, looking around.

"Yeah..."

"Did you get any sleep?"

He paused, wondering whether he should tell her about it, but he felt that to tell her would only make her as afraid as he now was.

"A little."

She smiled and they both got up, looking around. He picked up the blanket from the floor with her, folding it together neatly as she placed it into the backpack they were handed the night before, and stuffed it inside. Around him other people were already awake and Barnabe and his father were at the doorway. Both of them were waving him over.

"I'll be back in a minute Sophia."

"All-right."

They were waiting for him, but why, he was unsure. As he came over, coming to a stand near Kurubin, he began to speak. Several of the soldiers also stood nearby.

"I hope you slept well Graciou."

"Somewhat, yes."

Kurubin smiled, guessing he might very well know he hadn't, not to mention the fact that his eyes must have told that story for him.

"Well I'll get straight to it. We have decided to order the men into groups so we can cover everyone, just in case anything happens. But I think we should have someone at the rear as well."

"Sure, I don't mind taking the back, do you really think we will get attacked?"

Barnabe had been stood just outside of earshot and the others had fallen silent as he said it. Apparently Barnabe was not afraid to answer.

"Better to be safe than sorry I think Graciou. Whatever happened in there, it surprised us all to a great degree..."

He nodded, knowing there was nothing more to be said, especially to

Barnabe.

"When will we be leaving?"

"In a few minutes I hope, if everyone is ready."

"I will be ready."

Barnabe nodded, showing an air of foreboding as he did so and Graciou began walking back towards Sophia. She was busy helping the others with their things, moving some of the larger objects onto the carts.

"They want me to watch the back of the group, just in case anything…happens," he said as he walked over and she looked up at him.

"Still trying to keep you safe then?"

He smiled, knowing she was right and why he had not seen it for himself, he did not know. For it must have been his father who had decided to make him take up the back of the group. Nonetheless, he would do as he was asked.

"Yes, it would appear so."

Minutes later they had begun to move out of the chamber, into a seamlessly flawless backdrop, the snow glistening in the early morning sun. The sky was far bluer and freer from cloud than he had ever seen it. Even the landscape seemed sharp. A lot had changed since they had all been inside the citadel. Slowly, the long column of people began to move away from the snow-capped mountain. Kurubin walked back towards him as he shut the gigantic segmented door that was the fortress's entrance once more.

Before long he could see the long line of people weaving in and out of the pathway that he guessed Kurubin had taken him up the last time he was here. He watched as the ground now began to dissolve into darker and darker shades of long green grass. But as he now moved from the sharp cold air of the fortress out into the cool spring breeze, the questions of the previous night started to lift, only brought again into focus when Sophia spoke to him.

As the days drew on, they got closer to what had once been their home, each of them grieving for the loved ones whom they had been wrenched from so quickly. Most took the strength of his father and the journey they were now undertaking as comfort. He noticed as the day was growing late, that they were starting to file into a forest or clearing ahead of him. People had started to walk off into the two large forests, now able to see where it was they were going. He noticed this was the exact same place he had walked through before, just as he had met Kurubin. Though at that time, he had felt a sense of jubilation at being re-united with so many people, now his heart just felt heavy with the questions it had raised.

Slowly, the line came to a stop, they the last to arrive. He could see the mountain behind them, looking like it was being ravaged by a blaze of fire from the setting sun.

"We're going to set up camp here for a few days Graciou, I've told everyone to make themselves some sort of shelter."

He nodded, and his father seemed oddly cold for some reason.

"Let's go Graciou," Sophia said to him, as he walked on after her, into the quickly darkening forest.

Later that evening his father called him over to where him and Barnabe were sat. They had set up a small campfire in between the two large forests. He noticed there were pine trees all around him and the floor was littered with their cones. The place felt lush and damp, a dramatic difference from how he had felt in the Fortress.

Coming back to his senses he looked over at the fire, which in the short time had started to roar ferociously, warming each of them through and through.

"What's wrong?" he said, their backs still drawn to him.

"Sit down Graciou."

Quickly he sat and waited to hear what they had to say.

"We sent out a few scouts earlier on, to go ahead of us, make sure the coast was clear…"

"Why. Is it not safe?"

His voice carried some nervous tension.

"Oh no, it's safe, but it's the town. They said that it's in tatters, every brick demolished, the walls collapsed. Like a storm, on a scale they have never seen before, had produced such a force."

"Are they sure it's the storm?"

Barnabe looked up from what he had been eating.

"What else could have done it, to have destroyed the entire town like that? I think we shouldn't hinder the others with the knowledge of it yet, it will only reduce their morale more than it already is."

"What do you think father?"

"I think we should let them see it, as Barnabe says. To tell them now is only going to place everyone in bad spirits. At least, when we get there, we might be able to rebuild something of it. Start anew…"

The Storms of Acias

His father's words were as true as they always had been, words that no matter what seemed to happen, carried hope with them.

"We may yet still be able to, but we won't know until we get there. If you think we should leave telling them, then I agree to it."

"I agree that it sounds the best course of action."

"Then that is what we will do. We will depart in the morning, let everyone rest up first. Including yourself."

His father was not stupid it seemed, and knew he had not been getting much sleep.

"I'll do what I can."

He smiled, turning from where he had stood, the others looking sad about the news that they had overheard, but yet were prepared to carry on like his father had indicated.

For the rest of the evening, Sophia and he talked about what might come of the morning and he told her what the scouts had seen. She appeared upset by it, but at the same time, she appeared to take it as it came. As if worse things had happened than what he had told her. She was right though, worse things had happened, things that she knew had come of the past and things which only he could know of. She slowly nodded off beside him, nestling into his shoulder as she did so.

Though he tried desperately, he was again unable to sleep. Placing Sophia down onto the blanket they had laid out he got up, walking through the trees towards the edge of the forest. The trees hung like blankets overhead, masking an endless blackness that was surely behind them. The passage that split the two wooden outcrops in half was now shrouded in a thick mist.

He walked out into the centre of it, looking down toward where his father must still have lain resting. The soldiers had fallen asleep at their posts further away, as their chatter had diminished completely. Behind him he heard a ruffle, like the sound of someone stirring in sleep. But as he turned to greet them, he saw nothing and everyone was where they should have been. Then his eyes caught a flurry of mist, as it turned and tossed onto itself. Wondering who exactly had made the disturbance, he looked around.

"Hello?" he said.

But no answer came. No person or ghost appeared to move. Then as he looked down the path, he saw it. A figure of a man, barely any taller than himself, with a black dark coat wrapped around him, long shaggy hair down beside his neck, and clearly even from this great distance, a face that bore the signs of many a hardship.

"Who goes there?" he shouted to it, wondering exactly who this was.

"Come closer..."

It beckoned to him and with it's words he moved in closer, the mist slowly parting between the two of them, it's face now coming into view. Now standing barely feet from him, the figure looked dirty and un-kempt, he began to wonder exactly who it was, or had been.

"Tell me of your name stranger," he said, with a much stronger voice, some around him beginning to stir as they spoke.

"My name is Gracious."

His eyes widened briefly once more and then narrowed as his mind rationalised the thought.

"You cannot bear the same name as myself."

The man smiled slowly, then moved closer to him, the mist now fading ever more around them, the light beginning to hit the top of the trees.

"Oh I can, for I am, the same as you."

"You look nothing like me..."

Slowly he began to move backward. His father was now exposed behind the man, Barnabe nowhere to be seen.

"Looks can deceive all but the few who wish to truly see them."

"You speak in riddles."

"I speak of a language no other has yet heard," it said.

Graciou stopped moving, as it started to resemble certain qualities that the man who had spoken to him in the fortress had.

"Do you see me now?" it said slowly.

"I see a ghost before me."

More hurriedly Graciou moved away, the figure relaxing back into a more menacing posture.

"You perceive me as a ghost and yet I am nothing more than your long lost Captain." The figure had an air of desperation about it's voice, as if it thought it was somehow winning him over.

"Marcus was loyal to his family, not a betrayer of it."

"You suspect betrayal?"

"A betrayal by that of the one who commanded him."

Even from this distance he felt as if it's eyes grew with fire, as the mist began to fade completely around them and the trees to brighten.

"You are wiser than I indeed thought you ever would be Graciou."

Ahead of him, the figure began to change. From it's familiar form, into that of a dark shimmer, it's eyes piercing and haunting his own, it's white hands and nails sharp and ready, teeth bared like some monster. On the floor behind it lay it's host, cold as the day it had been taken and long since dead. Did it now think it would take him as it's new host? He did not believe the figures to be quite so erratic. They were as if scared by something, as if they were losing their grip.

"The force that once stood here alone, able to do as it willingly assigned itself, shall do so again. It will command the dignity and respect it deserves and YOU Graciou, shall FALL AWAY!"

As his last words were shouted, many began to stand up, looking around confused for an order. Men were beside him, most getting up to grab weapons, bullets whizzing in his direction.

"WAIT! Don't shoot it!"

They stopped, as his words had dictated, though some must have questioned why. Behind that of the figure, his father was standing. Barnabe still nowhere to be seen.

"TURN CREATURE!" his father bellowed forth from behind.

His sword was raised ready for him and in no less than a few seconds the figure had blown away from it's position, tearing toward him. Graciou wondered what he could do to help. Shooting at it would only kill his father. Quickly, he grabbed it's left arm as it lunged out, a pale angered face knocking him back down to the ground. His father swung forward with his sword, which was quickly blown out of his hand, smashing in half.

"BARNABE! WHERE ARE YOU!" Graciou shouted with all his might for him, wherever he was.

His father now tried to hold the creature off, himself. Kurubin was hurt somewhere and he knew he couldn't help his father, the other men incapable.

"WHY DON'T YOU JUST LEAVE HERE!" his father roared at it. "LEAVE US ALL!"

But his words appeared to make no difference. This figure, whatever it was, was much more powerful than the others had ever been. Above him, the sky was completely sodden in a dark brown twisted mass of clouds. Quickly thinking for the others around him, he reacted to protect them.

"INTO THE FOREST!"

Some screamed as they fled, others ran off scared to death by what they had seen, though most of the men for their bravery stuck to him, a rare few walking away.

He had not yet noticed, but the figure had stopped and his father was lying barely able to move underneath. He ran forward, quickly grabbing the figure and pulling it away. An overwhelming anger that had been building for how long he did not know, came cascading out of him.

His father now, lay limp on the ground, trying to move, a large and crushing gash in his neck.

"YOU DID THIS! YOU WILL LEAVE HERE NOW!" he said with ferocity in his voice.

Without the slightest thought the power had taken over inside of him, the creature had stopped attacking. He was not going to let it leave alive. He was now punching out at it, throwing it back against the trees and wrestling it, but nothing that he did seemed to be working. The other men watched from a contained distance, unsure what they could do, but guns were still ready to fire, at a single command. It's arms were now trying to free itself and it's face could barely meet his own.

"WHY DO YOU NOT FIGHT!?"

Roaring once more, his father's now half dead body was lying behind him.

A torrent of rain issued overhead just as he said it, hitting him all at once and with undignified precision, slowly turning the ground to mud.

"CEASE THIS NOW CREATURE!"

But it only appeared to make it stronger, as it freed itself from his now completely exhausted arms, walking back into the forest, each man opening fire, most missing horribly.

"We will meet again yet, Graciou, we will meet again…"

Slowly, it faded from view and he didn't bother waiting for it to do so, instead he covered his father's open wound at his neck, as he tried to speak.

"Son, I'm sorry, I could…"

"Don't speak, don't speak…" he said, his eyes welling into open pools, as they merged with the wet rain.

"Keep them safe son, keep them safe and make sure you make that girl the luckiest one alive…"

The choking was unbearable as his father grabbed for air, but none came. Slowly the twisted contortions of his body subsided and the light in his eyes faded, mirroring the dark brown clouds above, rain still lashing down over all of them. Was the Storm so senseless it would kill him that quickly? He knew what it was capable of, he knew its ways and yet, all he could ask himself was why? Why did it have to take him? The Storm sat fixed above them, relentless and unsympathetic.

"Ahhhh!" he cried out at it.

All that he could do was cry, cry as he continued to ask the question. His father had been taken so quickly, he hadn't even had a chance to stop the figure and even when he had fought it, he had not made the slightest bit of difference. If he could have done anything right there and then to have brought his father back, he would have, but the power of the Storm was too great. The rain continued to lash down from above, as if rubbing salt into an already painful wound, yet his hands remained clamped to his father's coat.

Laying his head down onto it, he slowly crumpled it under his fist, unable to stop the tears from overflowing from his eyes and cascading down over his hands.

21

Sophia emerged with the others from the forest after a while as he lifted his head from the body, barely unable to pull himself away. She rushed over to him, hugging him and pulling him toward her. Barnabe was running up the slope, finally he had appeared.

"NO!" Barnabe shouted, running even faster, limping from his right leg as he slid across the mud.

"What!" Barnabe shouted again, falling to his knees beside the body, trying to pick it up.

"We got attacked by a ghost," said one of the men who was stood beside them. Neither Sophia, Barnabe or himself could speak. He continued to clutch his father's body.

"It was so fast…we couldn't…"

The man stopped, unable to find the words to console any of them, nor to describe what had happened.

"Where have you been…?" he half shouted at Barnabe.

"I was scouting out ahead, checking that everything was all right for the morning. We agreed…damnit!"

"But I saw you, next to him, sleeping."

Barnabe stared at him in disbelief.

"I've been at the town Graciou."

Strengthening his tone he continued.

"I'm sure Barnabe, where the hell were you?"

"Hang on Graciou, you've got to believe me, I wasn't even here."

"How can you say that if I saw you?"

"Those ghosts can place devilish tricks on people Graciou, more than your mind can even imagine, please believe me?"

He was unsure what to believe at that current point. He felt as if he were floating and nothing around him even mattered.

"I know what I saw…"

Barnabe smiled at him, trying desperately to make him believe it was true, looking down at the body, openly sorrowful for what had happened and unable to believe it could have happened.

The Storms of Acias

"That figure will pay for this, if it's the last thing I do!" Barnabe whispered, in his own contained way, his anger boiling like a pressure cooker. But he knew better than Graciou that there was nowhere for it to go.

Hours went by before anyone moved, each of them looking as confused and unsure about what to do as the next. The very light around them was now a dark brown colour, creating an air of paralysing grief that consumed all of them.

"Barnabe?" one of the women said.

"Graciou," Barnabe said slowly and with great caution, gently lifting his hands from the coat. Graciou found himself surprised at how easily they now fell away. Then again, his body's strength was spent, though he doubted anything would take away the lingering rage he felt for the Storm, any strength he had to lead his people was lost.

"I'll take him Barnabe," Sophia said, picking him up by the arm, as she lead him away into the forest.

He felt her place him down on the bed where they had been sleeping, each of them sitting there, Sophia holding him to her. She had felt this before with her own parents and he felt her empathy without words or motion.

Barnabe came over to them later, some food in hand, trying to make up for his father's immediate death.

"I'm sleeping here tonight Graciou, you're not sleeping alone."

Barnabe hadn't meant to put Sophia out, but she knew Graciou didn't want to be alone. They each sat down as the night continued to fall on by, his gaze now staring limitlessly into the far distance, as he felt it would do for the entire night, were it not for the vestiges of tiredness, which eventually took hold of him.

His dreams were filled with figures and ghosts, haunting his every movement and blocking his every path. Nowhere it seemed could he now go, without stopping and seeing what was ahead of him. Then upon one of his paths he saw a man, standing with his arms by his sides and for a second he thought it was his father, but on second glance he saw it was not. Overwhelming anger spilled out of him as he launched towards it, beating it with his fists and causing no impact whatsoever, falling to his feet exhausted. But instead of disappearing or leaving him to the madness inside his head, the figure knelt, picked up his hands and raised his head.

"Do not be afraid Graciou, the pain will go and when it does, you will see the strength of your family within."

"Be watchful of the storm, for it will try to harm you and your people again. It has used nearly all of its power, but it will not take long for it to strike again."

Graciou continued to stare at him, his face was the same as before, the same as it had been in the fortress. Why was he here again?

"I do not have much time, for it is becoming ever harder for me to speak with you, but remember my words, remember what it is I tell you and use them."

But just as he felt his legs springing him back up to full height, the question was asked.

"Who are you?"

But the man merely smiled, as his vision blurred with a distant clouding in his eyes and a spark of thought in his mind and he was awake.

A startled Sophia woke beside him, his eyes already surveying the woods around, still pitch black. The morning sun had not yet rose and he guessed that it was only the middle of the night.

"What's wrong?"

"Nothing, go back to sleep."

"Tell me Graciou," she said, looking anxious.

"Someone spoke to me in my dream, he told me to watch out for the storm."

"It's just a nightmare Graciou, it's your mind taunting you."

But he shook his head, he knew it was not. She placed a hand on his shoulder, obviously worried.

"Are you sure you're all right?"

He looked at her face, unsure whether he was indeed well, but with her at least he had a point of reference with which to steady himself.

"No, I'd be lying if I said I was, but don't worry about me, whatever's happening I'll figure it out."

She smiled, kissing him softly, as she tucked herself back under the blanket to sleep.

Instantly his mind returned to the man who was in his dreams. He had been positive it was his father at first glance, but he knew it was not and yet he could not in his entire mind understand why he seemed so familiar.

The Storms of Acias

For much of the next day the storm lingered overhead, the longest he had ever seen it do so, the ground now covered in a thick brown mud bath. He dared not get up to face the body of his father, as if not seeing it would make the fact go away, but he stood none the less, determined by the words of his dreams, to stay strong.

Barnabe had his back to the wood, looking upward at the brown mass, which had shrouded much of the bright light of the sun from view.

"Barnabe?"

He turned slowly, looking like he had been transfixed on the Storm above. Slowly he turned to him, removing his arms from where they had been crossed upon his chest.

"How are you feeling?"

"Not so bad now I've rested." he paused "and you?"

Barnabe smiled as he spoke, his voice worn and tired.

"Sleep, what would any of us give for that. I shall be all-right Graciou, I have stayed awake through far worse, not to say that this doesn't affect me, because believe me it does."

"How long have you been stood here?"

"Oh, a few hours I guess, I like to keep an eye on it."

He referenced upward to the storm.

Graciou stepped forward, looking up at the heavy dark brown cloud and the river-like stream of mud, that was weaving it's way past them.

Then it came to him, like a question that would not go away, he turned slowly, looking over to where his father's body should have lain.

"Where's the body Barnabe?"

Barnabe turned round, looking over at the spot, quickly walking past him to get a better view. But sure enough, as his own uncle's eyes came upon the place where it should have been, it was not.

"It was right there, I only saw it last night."

Slowly he crept forward, to the edges of the forest, where he walked out into the slippery path, muddy water rushing past his feet. Barnabe was already out beside him, as above, the clouds toppled over on themselves and the dark brown gave way to brilliant white, illuminating the many forest ditches all around him. His father's body, barely metres from them, was half propped against a tree, mouth half open.

"Excem?!"

Barnabe cried, as he ran over to him, half amazed at what he might be seeing, but Graciou stood firm, not wavering in his stance.

"Graciou…I thought I was dead…"

But he knew what was happening.

"Graciou, it's your father…"

"I wish it was Barnabe."

"What are you saying?" Barnabe said laughing.

Beside Graciou lay his father's sword, which he picked up slowly in both hands.

"Graciou? What are you doing?" Barnabe said, as he stood there, weighing up what he might be about to do.

"Graciou, wait!"

Sophia's voice rang out, barely metres from him.

"He may look to be my father, but he is not, the figure that sits there is far from that person."

"Graciou, see sense!"

Barnabe shouted, this time trying desperately to stop what already appeared to be in motion.

But it was too late, picked up by some lustful hatred inside him, the same hatred he had for the figures, the nightmares, the storm's merciless anger, was now finally coming to a head. He plunged the cold metal blade down through the air, Barnabe flailing out of the way as he did so. But Graciou looked on, suddenly starting to feel more like a spectator than a person, he wondered who he was becoming.

The blade stopped barely millimetres from his father's chest. His skin was a cold blue and to the side of him, something stood.

"Very perceptive of you, Graciou."

Slowly his eyes looked around, to be met by that of the figure, the same ghost that had come to him in the castle and the same ghost that had taken so many of his people hostage.

"All this time, I've thought there to be more than one of you, but really, there isn't is there?"

If it could smile, then it was trying, the edges of its whitish lips, curling into a menacing edge.

"But there's one thing I'm beginning to understand. To fight, to gain my freedom and theirs, is what they want me to do. So that if I lose control of myself and my emotions they will be free to do as they wish, not just to me, but to everyone."

Placing the sword into the muddy ground by his feet, he stepped back, composing his mind and trying to regain his strength.

"Something's changed here figure, now I'm seeing what you truly are. Nothing more and nothing less than what your shell presumes to be."

It's smile still hung dauntingly, as if to pounce, but as his words forced dominance into the air, it shrunk to that of a child, with the inability to truly show it's power, with a coward's heart.

"Now we see you. All here see you! For what you truly are!"

It's smile faded, turning into a grimace that it could not permeate past his eyes or his ears. Graciou was seeing it for what it was. It may have had the face of the man who had come to him so many times, it may well have looked like so many before him, but he saw it for what it was, none less than the figure, reduced to its most desperate attempts.

"Do not dare to come back here again, because I won't allow you anywhere near my people!"

His voice remained calm as he had said it, and reduced to nothing the figure faded, into a shapeless ball of nothingness.

"Graciou?" Barnabe called to him, as if fearful for his sanity.

"It's gone Barnabe, it won't be back."

He hobbled over to the nearest stump where he could rest a minute, Sophia already beside him.

"Where did it go?" Barnabe said searching amongst the forest for some sign of it, unable in all his belief to understand where it had gone.

"I showed it who it was, no more than what it appeared to be, in truth, no more than a figure can be."

"That can't..."

"It is Barnabe, it's over, all of it."

But Barnabe still searched the forest, intensely.

"Too easy Graciou, far too easy..."

"Maybe Barnabe, but maybe we've all been looking in the wrong places, for the wrong things. When it was that simple all along."

Barnabe turned and walked away, all the others still trying to figure out who was speaking the truth.

Sophia still looked at him in partial awe.

"Do you believe me?" he said to her, making sure it was not just him that believed what he was saying.

"For as much as I can do, I believe you."

22

He woke with a start the next morning. Someone was stood in front of him, shouting down at him. A tremendous wind was rushing between the trees and battering the pines above.

"Graciou! Wake up!"

"Where has this wind come from?" he shouted back.

"I don't know, but Barnabe told me to come and get you both."

He nodded and tried to get up. All around him a raging wind was blasting through the trees, far worse than he had ever seen a storm whip up before. All he could see were blue skies and white clouds, the storm nowhere in sight. As quickly as possible they both got up and left, running as fast as they could to where Barnabe was stood.

"Graciou, over here!" Barnabe was shouting to him, standing just outside the forest, just beside the camp fire where they had been sleeping.

"We need to get to some sort of shelter, this wind is ripping through these trees."

He nodded quickly and glanced around, looking at the others and wondered where they might go.

"What of the castle Barnabe?"

"Yes, it will have to do, we will head there."

"Let's move toward the town everyone," Barnabe shouted once more, most hearing what he had said.

Hurriedly, he moved ahead with Barnabe, each of them moving off in the direction of the town, where he hoped there was still some shelter to be found amongst the remains of the castle. Up ahead of them the path opened out and the gate could be seen in the distance, toppled and broken. A large hole was set into the wall just a few yards up from it, which appeared to open out into the grounds of the castle.

"There Barnabe!"

He shouted toward Barnabe as he pointed at it, each of them following his lead, as they ran over to it, quickly and without hesitation.

"Lead on to the Castle Graciou, I'll wait here and make sure everyone gets through."

The Storms of Acias

The wind had appeared not to change, but walking across open ground had blown several of them over, though they were soon back on their feet.

The castle grounds were heavily overgrown, but what remained of the walls and plants had given adequate protection against the wind a fair few of the trees had already broken over with it's force. They each huddled around him as he tried to free the doorway with some of the other men. But no matter how hard they tried it was jammed.

"We need to find another way in."

He looked around to see Barnabe was already walking over to them.

"This way!" he shouted back as he began to move around to the side of the castle.

As they all followed, another large hole presented a means of entrance. Each of them huddled inside to find themselves within the entrance. The now largely disrepaired castle was in tatters, but at least it would keep them safe. Much of it was still strangely intact and he continued to move more of them inside as he looked around; each of the rooms appearing to be heavily damaged. He found it strange that of the entire town, there had been nothing left but the castle's grounds and the castle itself. Barnabe walked over to him, his face looked pale from the raging winds outside.

"I think that's everyone inside Graciou, do you think we can make shelter here?"

"Yes, this will do till the wind leaves."

Sophia walked in behind him, her hand finding his quickly, shaking slightly from the cold wind.

"Kurubin, do you think you can light some fires?"

He nodded, just about able to walk now on his leg, though it was taking a long time to heal he had managed to get it tended to.

Each of them sat down into their groups, as Kurubin lit the last fire for the three of them and they each sat down. Nearly straight away, he began to speak, unable to hold back the questions.

"I don't understand where that wind came from, one minute I was asleep, the next I was being woken up," Graciou said to Kurubin, who carried on stoking the fire in front of them.

Kurubin didn't answer, which he felt was strange for him. Barnabe had been at the back of the castle, pre-occupied, but now he was walking back to them, looking a little worried.

"What's wrong?" Graciou said as he walked over, watching him sit down before saying anything.

"The stairways intact, but most of the doors have been smashed in and most areas can't be reached, apart from some of the bedrooms. But what I do not understand, is why the storm would have left the castle like this, why did it not just destroy it completely?"

"It is strange, like the storm wanted us to come here. What do you think Graciou?" Kurubin said.

"I hope not Kurubin. We didn't even see where that wind came from."

Barnabe looked up from the food he had been picking at his eyes were full of confusion, which Graciou had never seen before.

Boxed in by the walls of the castle and the silence of the conversation, only a few questions remained at the foremost of his mind.

"This whole thing makes me uneasy," he said, openly to them.

"How so Graciou?" said Barnabe.

"It just feels strange, no storm, but yet the wind is as powerful as it was."

"And you suspect this is something else?" Barnabe said.

"I've been told to watch out for the storm, be careful to see what it might try and do next, if anything."

"Told by whom?"

He thought he would know that Barnabe knew him better than that by now.

"Not a figure, a man who has been speaking to me recently. He spoke to me in the castle, I may have spoken about him before."

Barnabe and Kurubin looked up as if they understood what he had said.

"What exactly did he say?"

"He said that I had to stay strong, I had to watch the storm."

"Well, I wouldn't worry Graciou, the storm's nowhere near us," said Kurubin once more.

"Correct Kurubin, but I think I may have seen this person myself," Barnabe said, Graciou looked over at him, wondering how that could be.

"Where?" said Graciou.

"He's spoken to me once before years ago. But the stuff he mentioned didn't seem worth hearing. Once I'd got past the fact that he wasn't a figure, I just couldn't understand why he was speaking to me about you."

"Why what did he say?" Graciou now said, eager to hear why Barnabe had never brought this up before and why he was so intent on disregarding whatever he had said.

The Storms of Acias

"He said that I needed to protect you, make sure you were safe. Not as if me and your father didn't know we had to keep you safe. I mentioned the prophecy, but it seemed he knew about that too. I never really gave any of this much thought, mainly because he seemed so out of place, but..."

The sudden image of his father came into view and for a moment he again remembered what had happened. A sickening feeling came into his stomach, but he pushed it away, focusing on their conversation.

"I'm not sure if it's the same person but," Kurubin looked frightened to even speak of it.

"You've seen it too?" Barnabe said hurriedly.

"Whilst patrolling outside on the mountain, we'd often seen a strange figure lingering at the edge of the blizzard, just within our vision. But he always kept his distance and so did we."

Suddenly, Graciou's memory was jogged and he could remember seeing the man in the silver chamber, before he had disappeared.

The conversation trailed off. It seemed the three of them had exhausted their will to develop anything more of what they had seen or discussed, even with the insight of more than one mind on the matter. But yet it did seem that something had culminated in Graciou's mind he knew that this man, whoever he was, could be trusted. But truly, who was he?

From the various openings in the walls the raging wind could be heard outside, not dissipating at any time as the sun dipped below the horizon, leaving a dark purple stain across the ceiling above.

"It's going to get cold down here tonight."

"Yes it will, but these fires should keep us warm."

Getting up he straightened out his clothes.

"I think I'm going to look around, see what's still intact," Graciou said, his mind looking for something to pre-occupy him, especially now that he was back within his home once more, or what he had once been able to call his home.

"Want me to come with you Graciou?" Barnabe suggested.

"I'd rather go alone Barnabe."

"All right, don't be long."

He turned and began to walk away through the wide corridor to the back of the castle, where the large canvas of his fifth great grandfather stood, now battered and torn by the rocks that had impaled the castle walls, yet he still looked down at him, the same stubborn strength swirling in his eyes.

The staircase still bore the signs of those that had been crucified here, years previous to the day, as he had fled with Mary. But the castle, even though dark and torn, still had within its walls a feeling of home. Slowly, he carried on up the staircase and towards the two large oak doors that opened out into his father's bedroom.

The doors still looked the same and the smell of oak filled his mind as he pushed them open, the buffed brass handles sliding easily away from his hands. The room looked the same as it had years ago. His mother's chest was barely touched, when once it had been tended to every day by Mary's own hand, now it lay dusty and cob webbed.

The same clothes hung in the wardrobes and the same smell emanated from them. To the far end of the room the two openings to the twin balconies were open and were blowing a now steady stream of air his way. Captivated forward now to a view he had not seen for so long, he wondered what exactly might have changed in all this time, if indeed anything at all. But even though his memory had been dimmed, he still remembered it.

"Barnabe said you might be here."

Quickly he turned, to find Sophia stood in the doorway, looking as beautiful as ever. But even her presence could not stop the tears from rolling down and off his cheeks, as the memory of his mother was brought to the forefront of his mind.

"What's wrong?"

"This was where she stood, where I saw her..."

His voice trailed off as he sat down on the bed, unable to stop the tears.

"What is it?" she said, coming over to him.

"I'd forgotten it until today."

"Your mother?"

He nodded.

"Is this where...?"

"I can remember the day, she was stood just in front of my cradle, I was looking out behind her at the sky," he paused, as slowly more of it began to come together in his mind. "She only turned round for a short while, stepping out onto the balcony, but already I had my eyes set on what was coming from the distance. So young..."

"I hadn't seen the storm until that day, but when it came like that, I was stupidly perplexed by it, unable to take my eyes off the objects as they began to rain down."

He stood up, looking out toward the place where she had fallen, the balcony now much smaller than it had once been.

"Graciou?"

"My father came rushing in, gun in hand, ready to fight off whatever it was. The maid had screamed from behind for someone to help and all I could do was scream out in terror as I watched."

Now a subdued sadness came over him, he felt as if his mind were numbing as he pushed the cotton drapes apart, walking out onto the balcony.

"You've taken everything I ever loved Storm, now I know what it is you truly desire!"

He roared out at it, the now darkening skyline shimmering back towards him, like a wolf within the woods. But was that wolf so placid as to stand by and watch once more, as his angered eyes scoured the clouds upon the horizon. He knew it would not he watched the horizon as the storm began to break apart, flying off haphazard in all directions, raging into an abnormal size, as it raced towards him.

"Graciou! Come back inside, please…"

He could feel it rushing toward him as if it was the same as last time, but this time he was ready for it, as slowly it circled overhead like a serpent ready for it's attack, funnelling down before it would send the same injustice that had met his mother. Yet, was this what he really wanted? Or had the storm only carved this path for him, his every move guided to this moment?

He could see it falling down from the clouds, defying reality once more, as it shot out from the base of the clouds and arced its path of destruction back his way. Then it happened, some part of him probably knew it was going to, but it hadn't been ready. He watched Sophia fall away from his view, as his body was torn from where it had been stood upon the balcony and thrown into the castle wall behind him.

"GRACIOU!" he heard Sophia scream, as his mind slowly descended behind a dark veil that he knew no name for.

As he lay there, completely numb and waiting on whatever it was that should now surely come so fast, he felt a warmth around him.

"Give me your hand," he heard from somewhere close by, yet there was no one there to meet him, just a hand dangling near to his view.

"I feared it might come to this, but I know what I must do."

Around him he felt as if the very air had become light, his body seemed to remould itself as it took on some strange new form. He felt the hand firmly grip his own.

"Don't ever give up, no matter what it throws at you. Where you find yourself you will be safe. The young man will help you to confirm what you believe, until the time is right. I give now to you, all I can, use it to protect the Gracious ones use it to protect yourself."

With that, there was a definitive shriek all around him as he heard something much like Sophia's pained voice breaking through, before his entire body became calm and serene, his mind descending into unconscious sleep.

23

"Where am I?" were his words as he opened his eyes, not at first noticing the darkness that surrounded him.

"Where is such an inconsistent word," a voice from close by spoke softly.

"Am I dead?"

Graciou tried to look around, but he could see nothing but blackness.

"Not dead, much alive."

"Then who are you?"

There was a pause, silence filled his question.

"Gracious did a brave thing doing what he did."

"Gracious?" Graciou enquired, wondering who this man was.

"The man who has protected you now for so long, such a merciless act…"

"I do not understand."

"Do you remember who it was that delivered the prophecy of Gracious?"

Graciou wondered where these questions were leading, for they made no sense to him.

"No I wasn't born yet."

"Well it was a man called Gracious who delivered it."

"Wait, I thought that the prophecy was set up to protect me?"

"Oh it was, indeed it seems to have done some of it's job."

"What do you mean some?"

There was another pause before it spoke.

"Because you are now here with me, and I doubt Gracious would have wanted that."

He felt himself go cold in the chair, all the small hairs on his arms standing up, for though he had a pretty good idea who this person was, he could not yet be sure.

"Where am I?"

"I see little reason for you to ask that qu…." His sentence was cut short, as a large shaft of light illuminated what seemed to be a room around him.

To his left something stood, and from the place where the light had appeared, he could see what looked like a man silhouetted.

"Ahh figure, you never cease to amaze me. Is this another poor soul you've got here ready for the host treatment?"

Another chill ran down him as the light was exhumed from the room and something walked in.

"What figure?" Graciou said, now knowing his first thought had been correct. He had not been sure, but it was a figure and it was stood near to him. Yet it should not have been here, it was dead. He knew it was nothing more than a ghost.

"He's not going anywhere," the faceless man replied.

To his right a massive ball of light blew up from the man's hand, it suddenly illuminated the room and indeed it's bearer. The man seemed young, his face was pitted with dirt marks and a light stubble covered most of his lower face. He noticed he was holding a cross in his hand, which was strangely similar to his own. Now he could see the man, he could also see the figure beside him.

"You!" Graciou shouted at it, able to see it had the same features as the other did it was that same thing that had killed his father.

"I've got it don't worry," the man said with complete satisfaction in his voice, as he walked over to Graciou, looking down at his hands. "Are you tied?"

He didn't much care about the bonds around his hands, he was more bothered about the figure.

"How can you be here? You stupid creature!" Graciou vaulted back at it again. How it thought it could appear, in any state he had no idea.

"Did I not say we would meet again?"

He ripped his hands free of the bonds, throwing the chair to the ground with a clatter the man stepped back, seemingly stunned as Graciou carried on toward the figure.

"There is no need to think me a demon in all this," it said, now sounding cowardly as he continued to move toward it. He found it strange now, how this figure could so easily articulate, when the others had not been able to, it's words were spoken like a well educated person.

"Just step back, I can vanquish him from the very dirt he stands on, if you step back."

"I know that, just give me a minute. I'm not done with him yet."

The figure for the first time seemed to grimace, as if nervous.

The Storms of Acias

"What are you going to do, you still haven't figured out how all this works."

"Don't be so sure..."

With reflexes faster than he had ever known possible, his hand shot forward, smashing into the figure's neck, as it grabbed his arm.

"Do you think more violence will solve what we have done?"

Graciou was now able to hear the fear in it's voice.

"I believe that for all you have done to my people that violence alone shall never be enough." He paused again before speaking. "But before I do snap your neck in two and kill you where you stand, I have one question."

Silence continued to run round the room as he stayed glued to the figure's face, it's two brazen white eyes trying to run away from him, yet unable.

"Well, ask it!"

"Why have you murdered so many of my people, what is your motive against me and them, why did you kill so many?"

Tears of fire were burning from his eyes as his entire heart reached forward for the answer. But it merely smiled as it answered.

"There are things you still have yet to learn about the game we play. We are not two players with intent to understand, we are one and the same player. We wish to understand the same thing."

Graciou gripped the figure's neck tighter, pushing it harder against the wall.

"Your time for riddles is over, tell me what the hell you are doing here!"

"I am here because I have been searching for Gracious, to find and kill him, before he got to you."

Got to him? What the hell did it mean?

"But you have failed," Graciou now said, staring at it's two white eyes, which had lost their hypnotic quality all together. It only smiled as it replied.

"We may have failed this time, but we have all eternity to make sure that we do not fail again."

"ENOUGH!" he heard from behind as the man stepped forward slamming his fist into the figure's head, splitting every part of it into smaller and smaller pieces, before finally it rotted beneath his hands.

"No, wait!" Graciou shouted, still wanting to understand it's riddle further. It made sense enough, but still it spoke as if he knew nothing, as if behind all this, all the things the figure had done, there was something else.

He now noticed the young man seemed to be staring at his face.

"My God, did it attack you?"

Graciou wondered if it might have happened whilst he was unconscious, but he was fairly sure it had not.

"Not that I know of."

"Your face is all torn and bruised."

Torn? It made no sense why his face should be torn, for he had not sustained any sort of injuries to his face.

"Here," the young man handed him the cross, which he turned over revealing a shiny buffed metal plate on the back. Graciou put a hand out bending the cross back and forth so that he could get a good view of his face, but the face did in no way match his own. Lifting his eyes up he stared at the man, then back at his reflection.

"I've seen a figure do worse," the young man said.

Graciou shook his head, for he knew it was not a figure that had done it. Indeed he had seen this face before, many a time and each time it had been cut off from him within seconds of it being able to deliver it's message. It was the face of Gracious, so heavily beaten no doubt because of his encounters with the Storm, encounters that he must have won within an inch of his life. Now what the figure had just said made more sense, for what Gracious had done was beyond what he had been able to see, far beyond himself, stretching to a place he felt his mind might never reach.

Graciou stood there, going over what the figure had said, trying to make sense of it. It should have been a final mystery, but with his body like this, the questions seemed endless once more.

"So I'm guessing he dragged you down here," the young man asked.

"No, no I don't know how I got here."

The young man rolled his eyes, as if he had seen it a thousand times before.

"You're probably just concussed, your memory of it all should come back."

But Graciou knew it wouldn't, because he had not lost his memory, it was intact.

"I would never have thought it before now," Graciou said aloud, pondering what the figure had said.

"Thought of what?"

He had no way of conveying it to him, not in a way that he would understand the experience was his own. Gracious had sacrificed himself to save him and in his last words, he had said that he was giving him something. He had given him his form, one which he could use to protect himself and the Gracious ones, whoever they were.

"Nothing, I couldn't explain it even if I wanted to."

"I'm sure it will come," he replied.

"What is your name?" Graciou said changing the subject.

"My name is Graciou," The man answered back, looking a little confused.

How he could have the same name as him? That was inconciavable. But that all depended on where he now was. For Gracious had to protect the Gracious ones. Could this possibly be one of them? He had no idea.

"I once knew a boy who held that name," Graciou looked over toward the doorway, putting a hand on the young man's shoulder.

He understood now that the Storm, even though it had pursued him for so long, had failed in its attempt to achieve what it truly wanted. Gracious had managed to somehow bring him to a place that the Storm would never have wanted him to be.

"But this name is sacred, I mean it's...He can't have had the same name as me."

"He never would have thought it possible either, until today..."

"So what changed his mind so quickly?" the young man said laughing slightly.

Graciou smiled as he replied.

"A man he barely knew showed him that even though the worst things in life will try to hurt you, they can be overcome that if you try you can save those you love the most and overturn whatever it throws at you."

"Not quite sure I understand," the young man said, now looking confused.

Graciou started walking them both towards the door, opening it as he stepped through, gently closing the door behind him as he spoke.

"I will be waiting Storm..."